What if a choice that [...]
your entire life, was [...]

A NOVEL

IF WE MEET AGAIN

The Choice

Nicole Spencer-Skillen

FROM BEST-SELLING LESBIAN ROMANCE AUTHOR

ALSO BY NICOLE SPENCER-SKILLEN

Choose Me

Are You Still Mine?

If We Meet Again

If We Meet Again: The Wedding

Nicole Spencer-Skillen

IF WE MEET AGAIN

The Choice

#Megley fans, this one is for you.

1

Column 13 (Draft)

Falling in love is one of the most extraordinary feelings in the world. Especially when you get past the whole—*I'm going to stalk you on social media* phase—and the following—*What are we?* phase—

How did I not see it coming?

How did I—the journalist—whose job it is to find and report the truth, miss such a vital piece of the puzzle?

Week in, week out, I discuss the love lives of my fellow Americans in this column. I help rekindle old flames. I chase down decade old connections. I convince the inconvincible that there is someone out there for everyone—sometimes. Those relationships aren't always successful, but neither is my "lovedar".

That's right, I'm calling it "lovedar". My gaydar seems to work reasonably well. I have no issues spotting a fellow member of my community, but realising they're in love with me . . . That's a whole other ball game. Just to clarify, I am referring to one lesbian in particular. She happens to look incredibly attractive playing said ball games, even when she's sweaty and out of breath, in fact, that's 100% my favourite part.

I can joke about this now and air my embarrassing tale for the whole of New York to read because I realise I was blind to pretty much every signal—and there were *A LOT* of signals. I'm talking large flashing strobe lights and red neon arrows pointing directly at her head. They do say better late than never.

Suddenly, I was willing to try oysters at a restaurant, despite the illogical fear of getting vibriosis; it seems adventurous now. I feel like it would be possible to drive a car through the glass window of a skyscraper into another skyscraper without falling to my untimely death. Maybe *The Fast and Furious* gang were just in love too. The other day I even wore the one sweater I swore I would never wear in public again, why? Because she said it gave her "sexy vintage hippie vibes." I'm still not even sure what that means. I don't care.

In a nutshell, being in love changes you. Real love, the kind of love that produces enough dopamine and adrenaline in your body that every supervillain known to man could threaten to destroy your whole existence and you'd shrug your shoulders, pick up your boombox playing John Legend's "All of Me" and your picnic basket full of rom-coms and chocolate covered strawberries and fight them off with the power of love. Just picturing that is giving me heart palpitations. I have basically become a human version of the floating heart smiley face emoji.

Next week's column is going to be about all the ways YOU, the good people of New York, ignored what was right in front of your faces. I can't be the only one?

I expect juicy.

I expect dramatic.

I expect life-changing epiphanies.
My email is below; you know what to do.

The column was a moderate success with people in New York. Ashley's column was inclusive. She covered all ages, genders, sexualities and races. The column was the only reason she'd been able to up and leave work at such short notice. When you ask your boss with one day's notice to take two weeks off so you can chase after the woman you love, they're going to give you one of two answers. Luckily for Ashley, Sonia's had been favourable, even when she told her she wasn't chasing Madison, the woman she'd almost married two weeks earlier, but someone different. Her response, *That will make a good story*—ever the journalist.

There was a catch. The column had to continue. Between trips to the countryside, afternoon tea, fish and chips by the seaside and watching reruns of Mr. Bean, Ashley set a few hours aside to do what she did best.

The sun rose on yet another cold winter morning. The orange of the sun illuminated the blue in the distance. It was a rare joy watching the world come to life. She'd been in England for a week now, every morning she'd wake before the sunrise. She found inspiration in the calm morning sky. The sitting room on the second floor was her place of choice. It was quiet and set away from the occupied bedrooms that flanked either end of the house. From what she'd been told, it was rarely used; it was more of a nicety than a room with any real purpose in the Davies' home.

Ashley reached over her laptop, opening the window just a touch, enough to hear the birds chirping in the trees. The nature on display from the rear of the property was like nothing she'd ever seen. She was a city girl; all she'd ever known was highly populated neighbourhoods with very little greenery. England was the opposite; she wasn't saying the sunrise over the fields in the countryside was better than the sunrise along the Hudson River. They were both amazing in their own rights.

Every morning she watched Michael leave the house around 7:00 a.m. for his five-mile run. Megan joined him sometimes, but this morning he was alone. He would turn and wave as he took off down the gravel path to God knows where.

Megan's parents had welcomed Ashley with open arms and no questions asked. It was like they'd known Megan would turn up with Ashley in tow at some point, and everything in the world would make sense.

A gentle arm wrapped around Ashley's chest. Then a face buried itself deep into the side of her neck, kissing slowly, softly. It was a greeting she could wake up to every day. The fall of Megan's hair draped across Ashley's shoulder; the smell of her perfume filled Ashley's head with a sweet jasmine aroma. It was Megan's smell now. Legally it was Louis Vuitton's, but to Ashley it was Megan. The way the perfume settled on her body made her skin impossible to resist. It made Ashley into a pheromone crazed animal, instantly aroused by the smell of her mate.

"Hi, you," Megan whispered, just below her right ear as her face nuzzled in the open space. Ashley rolled her head back, lapping up the contact she'd been so desperately craving.

"Good morning."

"What are you working on?" Megan whispered; every word that left her mouth sounded slow and sensual.

Ashley inhaled, closing her eyes gently, feeling the warmth of Megan's breath on her neck.

"I . . . just next month's . . . column." Ashley reached her hand backwards wrapping it around the back of Megan's head, running her fingers through her hair, and tugging as Megan continued to move her lips over her neck. Megan slid the thin checked shirt off Ashley's shoulders; it was the only thing separating her torso from her lips.

"Do you want to tell me about it?"

"No," Ashley muttered.

"No? Why's that?"

"Too much talking."

"If you don't want to talk, what do you want to do?" Megan teased. She reached forwards, one hand caressing Ashley's left breast, the other supporting the weight of her head as she rolled back and pursed her lips.

"Kiss me." Ashley exhaled.

The weight of Ashley's body was no more. Her muscles were loose, free. In Megan's embrace she felt alive. The warmth of Megan's body pressed against Ashley's shoulders as she turned her head to bring their lips together.

Is this what it feels like? Ashley thought. She imagined floating on a cloud to feel much the same. It was a surreal feeling, but one that clarified her decision as the right one.

The strong, almost inexplicable, desire she felt for Megan in that moment was impossible to control. The taste of her lips allowed her to forget their whereabouts for a brief period. *Almost.*

"Shit . . ." Ashley fumbled for the edge of her shirt.

"What?"

She spotted Michael making his way up the driveway. "Your dad."

"That's what you're thinking about?"

"No, idiot. Your dad just got back." Ashley shot forwards in the chair, breaking the intimacy. "Do you think he saw us?"

"I hope not." Megan chuckled.

"Why is that funny?"

"Come on, it's a little funny." Megan smirked.

She'd forgotten about that smirk. It was another thing to add to the long list of reasons why Megan was irresistible. The smirk was enough to get her to strip naked in front of the giant window without a care in the world, but that would be irresponsible. She had the willpower to resist. *Maybe.* Under no circumstance was she about to let Megan's father see her naked. But the *smirk.*

"Okay, stop that."

"Stop what?" Megan asked.

"That thing you do with your face, it's distracting."

"You mean my smile?" Megan found the whole interaction highly amusing.

"Yes, you know exactly what you're doing."

They heard Michael's footsteps bounding up the stairs. Ashley felt like she was going into cardiac arrest wondering if he'd seen her breasts. Megan seemed unbothered, She slowly ran the tip of her finger down the back of Ashley's neck.

"Stop . . ." Ashley murmured with no real authority. She was powerless to those fingers. She knew it. Megan knew it. Hell, even Michael knew it. It had only been a week and Ashley was completely and utterly defenceless.

Thankfully, the only thing she had to defend herself against was a woman who made her whole body vibrate. Every touch felt like a giant orgasm. The thought made her body quiver. It could be worse.

"Girls . . ." Michael's voice came from the other side of the door.

Oh God. Ashley swivelled the chair around, fully focusing on her laptop, and began typing away as though she hadn't just been delightfully groped for the world to see. Well, for Fred the shire horse to see. And potentially the chickens. Did birds count? Flowers? They were living organisms. They grew, ate and drank, if so, the groping had been quite the spectacle, Ashley thought.

"Yeah, Dad?" Megan perched on the edge of the desk, completely casual, unconcerned. Was she used to being caught groping her girlfriends? That was a question for later, Ashley noted.

"Can I come in?"

He'd definitely seen her breasts.

"Yes."

The door creaked open. He stood with a bottle of water in hand and headphones around his neck. Beads of sweat dripped from his forehead. He wore a compression vest that was so tight all he needed was a giant *S* and a red cape, and he'd be Superman.

"Morning girls."

"Morning Dad, nice run?"

"Oh yeah, perfect. What are you girls doing today?"

Michael looked Ashley directly in the eyes and didn't look down at her chest; they were in the clear.

She looked to Megan for the answer. If it involved anything other than a morning in bed soaking up every inch of her body, she wasn't interested.

"I don't know actually." Megan shrugged.

"I have an idea."

Megan eyed him suspiciously. "I already told you Ashley and Mom don't want to play two on two in the yard."

"Basketball? I never said I don't . . ."

Megan interrupted, "Trust me. You don't."

"Don't worry, I don't take it personally. She hates getting beat by her old man," Michael voiced.

Megan launched a cushion in his direction.

"I was coming to see if the two of you wanted to join your mother and me at a work gala tonight?"

"A work gala. Sounds fancy. What's it for?" Megan placed a hand on Ashley's shoulder; the delicate touch made her swell with pride.

"Just a celebration. It's been a successful year. We've invited all our stakeholders, clients, contractors etc. I know you probably want to do your own thing, but I didn't want you to feel like you weren't invited. We would obviously love to have you both there." There was an emphasis on *both* that made Ashley grin.

"That depends."

"On what my little girl?" Michael was just as sarcastic as his daughter and Ashley loved that.

"Is there a free bar? And have you got the caterers to serve up those cute little smoked salmon and cucumber canapés?" *Really?* Cute canapés were her bargaining chip? Ashley laughed.

Michael rolled his eyes. "You've asked about those canapés since you were thirteen years old."

"Have you ever seen another cucumber slice cut so thinly that it rolls up like a piece of ham with the most perfectly flaky salmon inside? No. We tried, remember? That woman was a genius."

"Yes, I remember your mother trying to replicate them for almost a year and you judging them like a very small, less hairy version of Simon Cowell."

Ashley burst out laughing. "Okay, that mental picture is a lot."

Megan turned back to her dad. "So . . ."

"The canapés are going to be great."

"But . . ."

"No, they're not salmon and cucumber rolls."

"Hmmm . . . then I'm going to have to think about it."

Michael launched the cushion back in Megan's direction. She dodged it and watched the circular object crash into a glass of water perched on the edge of the desk.

"Uh Oh," Megan said as she watched it tip over and spill all over the floor.

"Clean that up, Meg." Michael smirked. That's where she got it from. *It all makes sense now*, Ashley thought. "Ashley, you're more than welcome alone if my daughter can't get over her obscene canapé issues." He winked and swiftly departed.

"Did I tell you I love your dad?" Ashley slouched back in the chair. Megan removed her t-shirt and began soaking up the water from the floor.

"Yes, you did, yesterday actually."

Ashley recalled the hilarious incident. They'd stopped off at the local store to buy some fish food. Michael loudly instructed Megan in front of the store assistant not to eat it all at once.

"I think he's brilliant. I wish my dad and I had that kind of banter."

Ashley closed the laptop. Watching Megan clean up the water in nothing but her bra was much more entertaining.

Ashley spun the chair around, so she faced Megan with her legs straddling either side of her crouched body.

"Come here to me," Ashley whispered.

"Does watching me clean up water turn you on?"

"Watching you do anything turns me on."

"Oh really?"

Megan used the arms of the chair to pull her body up. The shorts she had on sat low enough to emphasise the carved lines of her pelvis. Ashley reached out tracing the muscle defined lines around her stomach.

"Jesus," Ashley whispered.

"What?"

"I think we should go back to bed, and I'll tell you all about it."

Megan pressed her tongue between Ashley's slightly parted lips. "Yes, please."

2

Ashley

The trip to England was Ashley's first. After a few days it became apparent that, yes, it did rain all the time. Not everyone spoke with an educated upper-class accent, and not everyone had met or was a relative of the queen. Apparently, the latter was quite uncommon. Ashley felt embarrassed when she'd had to ask Megan what *bagsy* and *doddle* meant after a conversation with her old friend from high school. *Why not just say, easy? What kind of word is doddle?* After the word was brought to her attention, Ashley had used it at every opportunity. The British language had some strange words, but who was she to judge? Megan was quick to point out English people thought the same about the American language.

On arrival, Megan's mom had asked about Ashley's BBL. Naturally, she'd assumed they were talking about the British Basketball League. It turns out Amanda had been referring to her British Bucket List. Ashley told them sarcastically that Megan's terrible timing and last minute invitation to fly halfway around the world with her had given her no time to plan a BBL. In the week she'd spent with Megan and her parents, Ashley came to know their good intentioned way of poking fun at each other. The common behaviour explained why Megan's level of sarcastic acceptance was at a ten.

After the conversation she got to preparing a list. They'd already visited a traditional British pub. Many in the US were made to look like them. The real thing didn't disappoint. They planned to take a trip to London to visit 48 Doughty Street—the home of Charles Dickens, where he'd penned his famous novel, *Oliver Twist*. It was now a museum. Ashley was a huge fan of his work and put it towards the top of her list. Megan suggested Chatsworth House. She'd never been, despite it being a location used in the *Pride & Prejudice* movie. Ashley planned to soak up all the literature she could by visiting the inspirations and locations of its creation.

Megan's only request was a trip to watch Leeds United play football. It was a ritual whenever she visited England. Ashley realised they were talking about soccer when she discovered that the game didn't involve twenty-two players with helmets, shoulder pads and an oval shaped ball. The atmosphere was amazing, and she enjoyed it none the less.

That afternoon, they found themselves at the York Designer Outlet. After agreeing to attend the gala, they had roughly three hours to find something suitable to wear for a black-tie event.

"I don't think you're going to find a dress in the Nike store," Ashley expressed.

"You don't know that." Megan smirked.

"No, I'm pretty positive you won't."

"What's this then?" She stuck her tongue out like a child. She held up an item on a hanger.

"That's a longline t-shirt."

"Looks like a dress to me," Megan said.

"Just to clarify, you're going to wear a Nike t-shirt to a black-tie event? Maybe you could wear your new Jordan's too?"

Ashley clutched Megan's arm and proceeded to drag her from the store.

"It could work; they're all black, with just a touch of white on the bottom."

"You're an idiot."

"You love me though."

Yes, I do, Ashley thought. She'd told Megan she loved her at the airport, in the heat of the moment. The declaration had been adrenaline fuelled and off-the-cuff. Immediately after having said the words, she'd felt guilty. Since then, she'd refrained. When Megan said, "I love you."

Ashley said, "I know."

When Megan said, "You love me though."

Ashley said, "Yep."

At first it hadn't registered, but now she felt the pressure. The guilt that came with declaring your love for another woman. Megan wasn't just any woman; Ashley knew it. Megan was *the* woman.

"Where to now?" Ashley asked.

"We can try Reiss; they usually have some unbelievable dresses."

"I am all for watching you try on dresses."

"I bet you are."

Ashley watched Megan make her way through the store like the Tasmanian Devil. She searched every rack in fewer than ten minutes. Eight dresses narrowed down to four. Ashley wasn't as versed in the world of dress shopping, but eventually she found a sleeveless tuxedo style dress. The second the satin touched her bare skin she knew it was the dress for her.

She sat on an incredibly comfortable cream velvet chair at the entrance to the fitting rooms. The assistant had been extremely helpful until they were six dresses in; then her genuine smile turned false.

"I think she's surpassed her customer service limit for the day," Megan said. Ashley chuckled. She could sympathise.

"Meg, can I see?"

"Two seconds. I'm just putting the heels on."

Megan emerged from behind the grey curtain; the black dress was the last option. The jersey fabric gripped her body; the V neckline emphasised her breasts. The floor sweeping dress had a thigh slit that revealed just the right amount of skin, elongating her tanned, toned legs in the process. It was sophisticated, sexy and sultry. It was everything Ashley saw Megan to be.

"Wow."

She twirled one way and then the other. "What do we think?"

"Wow."

"So, you like it?"

"Wow."

"Are you broken?" Megan laughed.

It took Ashley a moment to answer. "Sorry. You look . . . unreal."

"I think this is the one. I love the split down the leg. It's just enough. Not too provocative."

"I completely agree . . . It looks seriously . . ." Ashley glanced at her phone which was lighting up beside her. ". . . Madison."

"Excuse me?"

Ashley froze. "Madison just texted me."

"Oh."

"Yeah."

The moment was always going to come. The last text message Ashley had sent was two days before she'd left for England. Madison had no idea she'd left the country.

"What does it say?"

Ashley read the text aloud.

"Maybe I made a rash decision. I should have given you the chance to explain. I think I just needed some time to clear my head. Can we talk? I'm ready to listen if you still want to explain things."

***

When they returned to Megan's parents' house, Ashley made a beeline for the bedroom. She'd tried to call Jason. No answer. Getting a hold of Emily on a Friday was darn near impossible.

She'd snapped at Megan on the drive home, which she really hadn't wanted to do. They were only seven days into a fresh relationship. All she wanted to be doing was ripping Megan's clothes off with her teeth and praying they never had to leave the heavenly sanctuary they'd created in bed.

The weight of Ashley's body propelled her backwards onto the bed. Like a game of trust fall she opened her arms wide and flopped. In middle school there hadn't been a large comfy bed to catch her as she fell. That incident had resulted in a broken arm and two kids she no longer wanted to play with.

She scrambled to pull her phone from her extra tight jeans. They fit like a glove but were severely impractical.

Please be Jason calling.

"Hi," Ashley answered.

"Bambina. Sorry I missed your call I was out gathering items for the bar's gay night extravaganza."

Jason had been prepping for the launch of his bar's first pride night. If successful, it would become a regular monthly event on the calendar.

"Did you get what you needed?"

"I got rainbow tassels, foil balloons, flags obviously, glow sticks, personalised tattoos to use as stamps on entry, a giant rainbow piñata, horns, and the guy's number at the checkout." Jason paused to catch his breath. "His name's Chase. He's my height, has really cute arms and he has a jawline to die for."

"He sounds like an Abercrombie model."

"He gives his free time on weekends to do face painting for children with disabilities."

"I like Abercrombie. He sounds sweet."

"Anyway, what did you call me for? Did Megan forget to tell you she loved you this morning? And now you're wondering if she loves you at all?"

"First of all, that's rude. Second of all . . . I don't have a second of all." She'd already lost her train of thought. "Basically, Madison texted me and I don't know what to do."

"I know."

"You know?"

"She texted me asking if she should text you."

"Great, thanks for the heads up."

"Would a heads up have made you any less erratic right now?"

"Yes."

"Hmm, I beg to differ. So, what did she say?"

Ashley read the text out word for word.

"Huh."

"What?"

"Well, I can see why that would make you freak out."

"I'm not freaking out!"

"Really? Your voice is high pitched, your breathing is irregular and I can hear you fidgeting." She stopped toying with her belt buckle.

"Okay, what do I do?"

"I'm assuming she doesn't know you've left the country to chase after the girl you said you weren't in love with?"

"No."

"I'm also assuming she isn't completely insane for thinking that, just maybe, there could be a chance for the two of you to get back together?"

"No."

"And I'm assuming . . ."

"Jason!"

"Okay, there is no easy way to say this . . . You're fucked."

"That's fantastic."

"Although . . ."

"Yes?" She perked up.

"You could just say you lost your phone. Pick this back up when you get home next week, and you don't have to mention the fact that you ran away to England two weeks after your wedding."

"If I don't reply she's going to call you straight away and ask why I'm not replying. Are you going to say I lost my phone?"

"No, I don't like lying. It makes me feel dirty inside."

"Sooo . . ."

"Right, bad idea. I think you might have to reply."

"You think?" She placed the phone on loudspeaker and started pacing the room.

"I can't tell her over text, can I?"

"No. I wouldn't recommend it."

"Maybe I just keep it vague, and I'll tell her we can catch up next week?"

"Yes, but don't make it sound like you're going to grab a coffee with an old friend. She was almost your wife."

"Okay, so don't call her *buddy* then?"

"I'd advise against it."

Making everything into a joke with Jason was the only way she knew how to compartmentalize a stressful situation. The last thing she wanted to do was hurt Madison. She loved her. She would always love her, even if it was just as a best friend.

"Great, so send a casual inconspicuous text to my ex-fiancée—check. Now, I have to apologise to Megan."

"What did you do?" Jason sighed.

"I snapped. She was trying to tell me how to reply. She wants me to tell her the truth. I said it wasn't a good idea. She thinks I'm avoiding telling her because I'm unsure if I made the right decision."

"Huh, and what exactly did you say to that?"

"Just that it was my decision how I choose to tell her."

"Right. And you said it just like that? All calm and cool?"

"I might have been a little more irritable." It was the understatement of the century.

"Yeah, I figured. Do you want my advice?"

"Well, that depends. Is this like the time when I wanted to get a mortgage and you told me that it would take thirty years to pay it back, but if I just robbed the bank on 8th Avenue I could be out of jail in ten with good behaviour?"

"That's still true."

"Or the time I told you I was annoyed that I had to start paying my student loan debt and you said I should just fake my own death?" Those were just two examples of Jason's bizarre advice. They were all logically true if you had the lunacy to follow through with them. Ashley had a smidge more common sense.

"I'll have you know my cousin Lamar did it and he hasn't paid a dollar since."

"Lamar also only has two front teeth and refuses to go to the doctor for the pain in his back because in the eyes of the law, he's dead." Lamar was phenomenally senseless, but if someone asked Ashley to write a biography, he'd be the first on her list.

"It's not Lamar's fault his mother only fed him candy and soda as a child. Anyway, I think we're getting a little off subject."

"The stories about your family get more bizarre the longer I know you." For the first two years of their friendship Ashley had assumed he was making them up. Then she met Jason's mother. She'd threatened to give him an *ass-whooping* if he didn't help his uncle Tyrus drag the old washing machine out to the garage. That was within the first five minutes of their visit.

"Honey, you should have grown up with them. I'm surprised I'm the deliciously presented human that I am."

Ashley burst out laughing. There was only one person who could get away with calling themselves *deliciously presented* and not sound like the biggest egomaniac in the world.

"Please get to the point."

"Okay, I think Megan will be feeling a little uneasy. She knows you love Madison. You don't just switch those feelings off. Megan has been in love with you for years. I know it. You know it. Hell, the whole of New York knows it, but you denied your feelings . . . because . . . well, you're an idiot." Ashley didn't argue with that. "She needs reassurance. She needs to know that you flying eight hours across the Atlantic Ocean and declaring your love for her isn't something you're going to wake up and regret in a month's time."

"I know." Ashley huffed. "I have some making up to do."

Megan had been quick to go and feed Fred when they returned from shopping. Ashley observed the stables from the window in Megan's bedroom; there was no sign of her.

"You just enjoy your time there in your X-rated, picture-perfect bubble with that hot ass basketball player. Worry about all the other stuff when you get home."

Now, that was some advice she could accept. "Thank you. You're always there when I need you."

"That's what best friends are for. That and getting you out of jail."

"Let's hope you don't ever need to do that."

"But I would."

"I know."

"Text me tomorrow. You still haven't told me about all the sex you've been having."

"Okay, I'm going."

There would be absolutely no such disclosures. Some things were better kept between the two participants, which made it sound like a sporting fixture. Well, it did work up a sweat. The aim of the game was to score, and if you did it more than once you got bonus points. Her analogy wasn't too far wrong.

They said their goodbyes. It was time to get ready.

3

Megan

The past week had been one of those rare occasions when everything seemed to slot into place. Like in the final episode of your favourite TV show when all of the characters finally get what their hearts desire and live happily ever after. *Until the reboot.*

Cheryl informed Megan of a promotional deal with an up-and-coming fitness brand; they wanted her to be the face of their nutritional line. When she arrived back home in New York, a large batch of products would be available for her to try. If she'd learnt anything from her father, it was not to put your name to something you don't believe in. She would test the products before she started with any social media spiels about how they were the best thing since Beyoncé's 2018 Coachella performance.

The lease for her apartment had been signed. As much as she loved living with her aunt Julie, she wanted to reduce the forty-minute commute to Barclay's Center by moving into Brooklyn. She'd never lived alone and felt now was the time to establish some much-needed privacy. She was finally a fully-fledged adult.

The two-bedroom condo in Williamsburg overlooked the water and had stunning views of Manhattan at night, two things she'd added to her *do not compromise* list.

After a successful first season with the New York Liberty, Cheryl had informed her that a contract extension was definitely on the cards. That had been the aim, impress enough to get an extension for three or maybe even four years. She had no plans to leave New York. It was her responsibility to prove that she was an asset.

And, of course, there was *Ashley*.

Since their arrival in England, they'd spent every night in each other's arms. They talked about their hopes for the future, their fears, their feelings and what life would be like together. They didn't dwell too much on the past, only revisiting it for positive reference. They spoke in detail about their first date. Ashley noticed the photo of them kissing on the Wonder Wheel. It was attached to the mirror on Megan's dressing table. That sparked an awkward conversation, but all it did was solidify how long the feelings had been present. They laughed at the unfortunate timing of their past meetings. They recalled the baby shower incident where Megan had so desperately wanted to forget that her girlfriend at the time Candice existed, and the rooftop bar encounter when it took the power of God himself to stop their lips from brushing together.

They laughed at each other's jokes and cried at the numerous sickly rom-coms they endured each night. They smiled for no reason and danced around the room with the fluidity of two people who knew that what they had was special. They weren't about to audition for a new *Step Up* movie, but that didn't matter.

Ashley was always the first to drift off to sleep. Megan would watch the rise and fall of her chest. She'd trace her finger down the length of Ashley's exposed body. Sometimes she would wake up, and the intense, prolonged eye contact that followed only insinuated one thing. When they were alone together the sexual arousal increased with each intimate encounter; wearing clothes became a thing they did outside the bedroom. Inside it became pointless.

The bubble they'd emersed themselves in was *fantástica,* as Sofia would say.

Until that afternoon.

When reality stopped dragging its heels, and finally caught up with them.

***

Megan observed Ashley as she reached for a glass of champagne from the waitress. The event was flawlessly organised, and decorated, but Megan's mind was distracted.

"Can we talk?" Megan asked.

"I really don't want to get into it at your parents' event."

"I don't either. I just can't stand this." Megan waved her hand back and forth between them. "The tension. I don't like it."

"I know." Ashley breathed out heavily.

"Megan? Is that you?" The shrill voice coming from somewhere over her shoulder sounded familiar. *Oh.*

"Naomi, hi. What are you doing here?" Megan asked.

She leant in, placing a kiss lightly on each of Megan's cheeks. She tucked a glitter clutch under her arm and manoeuvred the train of her long golden dress to one side.

"My dad started working on a contract with your dad a few months ago. They extended tonight's invitation to the whole family. I wasn't going to come until I realised you were back in town."

Naomi Leigh was the sister of the power forward for the Manchester Mystics. They'd met at a few games and hit it off. After her relationship with Candice ended, Megan had turned her attention towards Naomi. She was single, attractive and known to be great in bed, which was ideal at the time because Megan didn't want anything serious.

"Oh. I didn't know that." Megan looked towards Ashley; her face looked sceptical.

"Naomi, this is Ashley."

"Nice to meet you." Ashley nodded.

"Is this your . . ." Naomi paused. *What is she going to say? Friend? Best friend? Business partner? Anything other than, ". . . girlfriend?"*

There it was, the word they were yet to discuss. They'd been at the event for approximately thirty minutes and Megan already wanted the ground to swallow her whole. *Now what?* Her mind raced. She could acknowledge the word or brush it off and make the situation ten times more awkward than it was already.

Ashley responded, "No."

Megan's heart sank.

Ashley reached her arm around Megan's back. She felt her hand grasp the left side of her waist and pull her closer. "We're so much more than that." She delicately placed a kiss on the side of Megan's face. Neither of them looked in Naomi's direction for a few seconds. They gazed at each other. *What did that even mean?* Megan didn't care. The gesture was enough.

"You two are literally the cutest."

She said it with the same sincerity that Regina George said, "I love your skirt," in *Mean Girls*.

"I'll leave you lovebirds alone. Megan, it was great to see you. Let's not leave it so long next time." Naomi ran her hand down Megan's bare arm as she passed.

Ashley raised an eyebrow. "Really?"

"She's harmless." Megan shrugged.

"She's something. You dated her? Like, seriously?"

"I never said I dated her."

"It couldn't have been more obvious. I'm surprised she didn't compliment you on your amazing biceps and how perfectly your hair curls." Ashley flicked her hair over her shoulder, mimicking the flirtatious gesture.

"Okay, thank you. I do work hard on my biceps in the gym. And, yes, I am incredibly lucky to have such curltastic hair."

"I did study literature, and I do write for a living. So, I'm pretty confident when I say 'curltastic' isn't a word."

"Can we just circle back to the bit where you claimed me? I prefer that part." Megan winked.

Ashley placed a hand on Megan's cheek, her thumb brushed the line of her jaw. Their bodies were now closer than some would deem appropriate for a public event.

"How long do we have to stay?" Ashley whispered.

"I think an hour should suffice."

"I don't think I can wait that long."

***

The cab ride home was torture. The idea of getting caught being intimate in public thrilled Megan, but she was positive it could result in jail time. So they held out. The PG exchange involved caressing hands and staring longingly. The cab driver's radio station of choice was Heart. When "West End Girls" by Pet Shop Boys came on, he glared through the rearview mirror and said, "You like this one, yeah?" Megan didn't have the heart to do anything but nod. He swayed from side to side, frequently making eye contact which helped to significantly reduce Megan's desire to rip Ashley's clothes off.

Time seemed to slow once they made it home. In the bedroom, Megan removed her jewellery. First she took off the sparkling silver tennis bracelet her dad had bought her for her eighteenth birthday. The ring Nancy had purchased for her twenty-first birthday followed, and finally the necklace. The delicate diamond necklace had been a gift from her mother after graduating college. Each piece had sentimental value. Unlike the jewellery, she didn't intend on removing Ashley from her body.

Reflected in the mirror, she saw Ashley begin to unbutton the double-breasted dress.

One button.

Two buttons.

The dress opened at the front to reveal the petite black underwear beneath. She wasn't used to seeing Ashley so feminine. The jeans and sweatshirt had been cast aside for an outfit bursting with sex appeal. Suddenly, she felt self-conscious. They'd had sex, every night since their arrival, but tonight was different somehow. Megan sensed a change in the atmosphere and she wondered if Ashley felt it too.

Megan watched Ashley make her way towards her through the reflection in the mirror. The movement from one side of the room to the other was like something out of a perfume commercial. Charlize Theron in the Dior advert came to mind; the thought only aroused her more.

They were face to face, breathing heavy.

"Hi," Megan mouthed. She had every intention of saying the words out loud, but they came out less than a whisper.

Ashley brushed the hair from her neck and leaned in to kiss below her ear. "Hi."

"You're killing me."

"Yeah? Why's that?"

"The dress . . . the underwear . . . the kissing . . ."

"Anything else?" Ashley teased.

"The kissing . . ."

"You already said that." Ashley moved to the other side of her neck. Slowly, but surely causing the heat to rise through her body.

"I felt it was important to mention that twice."

The soft touch of Ashley's fingers moved slowly up her exposed thigh. Ashley removed the shoulders of Megan's dress one by one, taking the time to appreciate every visible bit of skin. The dress dropped just below her breasts; with a little nudge from Ashley it fell all the way to the floor. Inside her mind, a small mariachi band applauded her for choosing the matching nude underwear set earlier that afternoon.

Ashley sat back on the bed, pulling Megan towards her. Megan straddled either side of Ashley's legs with her own. She felt exposed, her body on show for Ashley to observe, but as soon as she felt the hand crawl up her inner thigh, it didn't matter. The desire in Ashley's eyes was enough to reduce the nervousness, leaving only a sexual yearning.

"Lie back," Megan demanded.

Ashley smirked. "I like it when you boss me around."

Megan gradually made her way upwards; she sat with her legs around Ashley's waist, pinning her arms above her head instinctively. Her attempt at being *sexy* had historically gone amiss, but recently she'd felt a new level of confidence. Everything was different with *Ashley*.

"You're . . ." Ashley wriggled her arms free and placed a hand on either side of Megan's face; she kissed her lips with a gentle intensity. ". . . everything." Ashley used the weight of her body to force Megan over. Megan lay panting underneath a hovering Ashley.

Megan's body coiled tighter as her hands tangled in Ashley's loose hair. Ashley had been quick to identify what made Megan moan, and she knew what movements made her gasp. Those realisations had been apparent after their first twenty-four hours together. They'd explored the real depths of each other's bodies in record time. Megan desperately tried to inhale her next breath before she succumbed fully to the pleasure. She gathered the soft sheets on either side of her outstretched arms, creating knots in the fabric beneath her contracting hands.

The arch of her back allowed for ease of movement; the simple adjustment amplified the sensitivity. The rhythm of Ashley's fingers matched Megan's body's intensity up until the final thrust. She shuddered before granting her motionless physique a moment of serenity to enjoy the implausible orgasm.

How do they get keep getting better? Megan thought. *How is that even possible?*

After feeling the pleasure of her second climax, she returned the favour. They continued until they were both completely satisfied.

Ashley leant on her side, propping her head up with her left arm and slowly tracing the length of Megan's torso with her right.

"That tickles." Megan giggled. Shuddering from the feather-like touch.

"I . . ." Ashley paused. Her lips tightened.

"What?" She turned her body to mirror Ashley's.

"I love you," Ashley said.

Megan felt a sudden rush of euphoria. Her heart rate increased as her body felt the power of those three small words. It was the first time she'd heard them so sincerely; Ashley didn't break eye contact which amplified the intensity. The words felt like a rite of passage into a more profound intimacy.

"I love you too." Megan placed her lips upon Ashley's, confirming the words with a tender seal.

"I can't explain it, but you, us, it just feels real. It feels like . . ."

When she hesitated, Megan finished her thought. "It was always meant to be?"

"Weirdly. Yes. I'm sorry." She shook her head.

"What for?" Megan asked.

"For taking so long to realise it."

"We're here now." Megan brushed her lips against Ashley's once more. "I wouldn't change it for the world."

Megan knew that love wasn't always so cinematic in real life. It was challenging, consuming, ugly, heart-breaking, confusing, terrifying and so much more. It was a process that involved building a connection, trust and seamless communication over a period of time.

Love was allowing your partner to have the last bite of your favourite chocolate bar despite them saying they didn't *want* any chocolate. Love was attending your partner's family event despite knowing a huge argument was inevitable and that the evening would be long and painfully awkward. It was learning to forgive, to compromise and above all else to be present through the good and the bad. Megan wanted to experience it all with Ashley.

4

Ashley

The door to Ashley's apartment slammed shut. After hauling a suitcase, a hold-all and two duty free bags of goodies up the stairs she could barely feel her arms. She'd completely forgotten to buy Emily and Jason something. Airport souvenirs and alcohol would have to do.

The two weeks in England had been a welcome break. They'd been a brief stint away from the painful reality she'd left behind. It had remained in the back of her mind—waiting. The second she touched down on home soil, she felt the urge to escape on the next available plane. She could go for a remote island vacation, nothing but sun, waves and palm trees. *If only.*

"Thank God you're home." Emily stormed into the hall from her bedroom. No hello, that would be deemed too much of a nicety now?

"Why aren't you at work?" Ashley's confusion formed in the way of frown lines. It was a Friday, Emily never had Fridays off work.

"I booked the day off. I figured you'd need some moral support when you got home." She shrugged, as though it wasn't a big deal.

"You did that for me?"

"Technically, I did it for me because there is no way I would've been patient enough for you this evening had I spent the whole day organising Mr. Bexel's life."

Emily wandered over and wrapped her arms around Ashley. "I missed you."

"I missed you too," Ashley confessed.

Emily squeezed her tighter than expected.

"This apartment is boring without you."

That was suspicious, Ashley thought. "Did you kill the fish again?"

"Why would you just assume that?" She frowned. "And FYI, I didn't mean to kill Sushi."

"You didn't feed him for a week, Em."

"I Googled it and the internet said they could go three weeks, so I don't think it was my fault." She stomped towards the small square fish tank on the kitchen counter. "See, look he's flapping his little body around." She tapped on the tank. "I even think he's smiling."

"Fish don't smile."

"How do you know?"

"I'm almost positive they don't have a brain developed enough to smile."

"Whatever. Anyway, he's alive." She sprinkled some food into the tank for good measure. Point proven. "So, what you got there?" Emily snatched the duty-free bags from Ashley's hands. "Is this for me?"

"Some of it, but don't take all the best stuff. It's for Jason too."

"Would I do that?" She gasped, tipping the bag upside down on the table like a child at Christmas.

"Yes, you absolutely would." Ashley remembered the incident of two Christmases ago when they'd decided to do a December box with twenty-five individually wrapped presents. There was one for each day in December and then a special, more extravagant one for Christmas day. The gifts varied from a pair of socks to a pen or a book. The more creative the better. Emily sucked at gift buying. She also hated receiving because she couldn't lie. On Christmas day she went around each bag doing *swapsies*. That's what she liked to call rebelliously taking all of the good presents.

"What's this?" Emily held a giant bar of chocolate in her hands.

"Mint Aero, Megan said they're really nice."

"Okay, I like mint. That could work." She also grabbed the fridge magnet of Big Ben.

"Really? That can go in Jason's pile,"

"But the pen, I like the pen." She began scribbling on a piece of paper. "That's cute."

She unravelled a piece of tissue paper to reveal a red phone box style pen holder. "Perfect, I'll put my pen in there." Ashley hadn't expected her to like that one.

She threw aside a pack of mini mars bars and reached for the small cloth tote bag. "A bag with the queen on it?"

"I figured that was a Jason present, you know he loves the queen."

His obsession with the Queen of England had started after watching *The Crown*. Now he was insistent they were somehow related.

"I'm going to try some of this Aero. Want some?" Emily jumped up, ass first onto the kitchen counter, slamming the backs of her legs onto the worktop without so much as a flinch.

"No, it's all yours. You're welcome by the way."

"Thank you," Emily mumbled with a mouth full of chocolate.

"How are you anyway? No Sofia?"

"She's at work. I'm fine. Apart from having to pretend you're like president level busy so Madison doesn't turn up demanding to see you." Sofia had practically moved herself into the apartment after Emily agreed that they were officially dating—apparently the first five times they'd slept together didn't count because that was just a "trial period".

Ashley desperately wanted to be emotionally mature enough to deal with the Madison situation, but at the same time she wanted to fly back to England and change her phone number to avoid the conversation all together.

"Sorry." Ashley cringed.

"Do you know how hard it is to come up with reasons for you being so busy when you only have two friends, half your family lives in California and your job is Monday to Friday nine to five. It's not like you've got a ten-day summit with all the world leaders I can blame it on." Emily bit off another large piece of chocolate. "This is really good," she mumbled.

"Excuse me, I have more than two friends!" She crossed her arms, sulking. "And when have I ever worked nine to five?" The hours on her contract might have stipulated regular business hours, but that schedule was about as accurate as the weather forecast.

"The details are irrelevant at this stage. Last weekend though, I had to pretend like you'd gone to your mom's because she wanted to come over and speak with you."

"Oh."

"Yeah! I don't like being in this position. I have avoided her like the plague this week. She asked me twice to go for dinner, and I said I had to work late! I've turned into Meredith Grey."

"Oh, so now you're a TV surgeon who works eighty hours a week?"

"I might as well be."

Ashley scoffed and slumped on the sofa. It was good to be home. As much as she'd enjoyed exploring England for the first time, the fear of facing reality never fully disappeared. Emily was her best friend. Ashley knew that despite her love for Madison and how much she'd loved the two of them as a couple, Emily would always choose to support Ashley. It made facing the situation head on easier, but it also filled her with guilt. It had been the three of them for almost eight years. The thought of Madison no longer being a part of their trio pained her; it was like Alvin and the Chipmunks without Theodore. They were Charlie's Angels with Cameron Diaz; it didn't work.

Emily launched a piece of chocolate at Ashley. It bounced off her chest.

"Do you mind?"

"No." She jumped down from the worktop. "So, what are you going to do?"

"About Madison?"

"No, about climate change. Of course I mean Madison." Emily picked up the piece of chocolate that ricocheted off Ashley and blew on it for good measure before cramming it in her mouth.

"Should I call her?"

Emily gulped. "And say what?"

"I don't know . . ."

"I hope you had more conviction than that when you arrived at the airport to see Megan."

Ashley scowled. "That was different."

"How?"

"Because . . . I wasn't breaking her heart." Ashley dropped her head in her hands. "What if she wants to get back together?"

Ashley feared that the most.

What if she wanted to try again?

How did she tell her that she'd already moved on?

"Then, you tell her the truth," Emily stated.

"How? I can't do that to her."

"Do you love her?"

"Of course I do."

"Then you have to be honest, Ash. It's not fair for her to find out any other way."

"I know."

"Once the dust has settled, she'll understand." Emily seemed confident in that.

"Do you think?"

"Don't get me wrong, she'll probably light a match and burn everything you ever bought her, pawn her ring and slate you on social media, but once that's over and done with, she'll understand." Ashley had seen enough breakup montages to know how that went.

"What makes you so sure?"

"Because she isn't completely innocent in all this," Emily alleged.

Ashley sat forwards concerned but curious. "What do you mean?"

Emily rolled her eyes as though it was completely obvious, and she shouldn't have to explain herself.

"She knew all along that you loved Megan. She told me years ago. She told me before you asked her to be your girlfriend. She told me the day after you got engaged. She even told me a few weeks before your wedding. Madison knew that your heart was never fully with her. She would have rather kept you, even if it was only half of you, than let Megan have you. I think whatever way you look at it, there's no denying that it's a little selfish."

Emily placed the remainder of the chocolate bar on the coffee table. She sat down beside Ashley and clasped her hands together tightly.

"I haven't told you this. When Madison overheard your conversation with Megan at the wedding, she came and found me. She told me what she'd heard and asked if it would be wrong to go ahead with the wedding."

"Wait, what?" Ashley shot forwards. "She was still considering marrying me?" The thought made Ashley shudder. How different things could have been.

"Yes."

"Even after everything Megan said?"

"Yes."

"But, why?"

"This is what I mean when I say nobody is innocent. She was willing to sacrifice her own happiness and yours, for what reason? To prove a point? To say she won the girl?" Emily sighed. "That came out wrong. I'm not bad-mouthing Madison. She loved you and that was probably the overriding factor in her decision. She hoped maybe you would change your mind."

"What made her not go ahead with it?"

"I did."

"I don't understand."

"I told her she needed to walk away."

"You did what?" Ashley's tone switched. "Why would you do that?"

"Because it was the right thing to do, and I would do it again."

"Says who, Em? That wasn't your decision to make."

"What was the alternative? You get married and Madison stops you from seeing Megan. That puts strain on your relationship. She stops trusting you. You start sneaking around behind her back. It turns nasty, and eventually you get a divorce. Would that have been the better option?" She had a point.

"You don't know that it would've worked out like that." Ashley stormed to the fridge, grabbing the conveniently placed bottle of wine.

"I do, and you do too. This way, you get Megan. And maybe one day you can be friends with Madison again. The alternative would've resulted in losing them both."

Would it? The question she asked herself now was— *What if the wedding had gone ahead? Would that have been their fate?*

"I want to be annoyed at you," Ashley whined.

"But?"

"I fear you're probably right." She chose the biggest wine glass she could find, filled it and then guzzled the remainder directly from the bottle.

"I always am."

"I know, and it's extremely frustrating."

Emily walked towards the counter, eyeing the bottle of wine. "It's 10:00 a.m. Is the wine necessary?"

"My body is still on English time and it's 3:00 p.m. there. It's either this or we go for a run."

"Wine it is then." Emily grabbed another glass from the cabinet, and Ashley found a second unopened bottle in the fridge. "What's that saying? If you can't beat them, join them?" She wrinkled her nose.

"Exactly. Now, the question is . . ." Ashley held the bottle towards the bottom, gently pouring until the wine reached the widest part of the glass. The bartender within remembered the perfect way to pour to best savour the taste. "Do I really tell Madison about Megan?"

"God no!" Emily shrieked. "Are you crazy?"

"You just said that I should tell her because it's unfair for her to find out from someone else."

"I lied. It's not a good idea."

"Great!" Ashley threw her arms up in the air, she loved her best friend, but she also hated her best friend. According to the teen magazine she'd read on the flight home, that was completely normal. "I wish you'd actually just stick to the advice you give."

"Why would I do that? Then you'd blame me when it didn't go how you planned. I can't take that kind of responsibility."

"You're my best friend; it's your job to share the responsibility."

"I didn't fall in love with two girls," Emily said matter-of-factly.

"This time."

"That happened once . . . Okay, twice . . . unless you count the time I fell in love with Bette and Tina on *The L Word.* I couldn't decide which one I wanted to be with." *The L Word* phase was a dark time.

"Honestly, I'm so glad you're over that. It's not normal to watch reruns of a TV show every day consistently for a year."

"It is when your life is a disaster, and your only saving grace is Bette Porter in a tank top. Come to think of it, I think it's time I revisited the best six seasons of TV ever made."

In response, Ashley consumed half of her glass of wine in one swig. "Seriously though, I don't tell her?"

"I think you'll know what to do in the moment. It might be too soon to drop that bomb, but if she does want to get back together, how do you say no without a reason?"

Ashley said nothing, momentarily unsettled. There is nothing more frightening than telling someone you no longer want to be with them. Some would say it's a worse grief than death. When someone dies you no longer have to see that person. You don't have to split your assets or argue back and forth over text about whose fault it was or, worst of all, witness them move on with someone else. *Is it easier?* Maybe.

"I think we need to finish this bottle of wine. Then I need to stay awake until at least 5:00 p.m. to make sure I wake up tomorrow back on New York time. Then . . . I will text her."

***

The weekend was almost over, Ashley had spent most of it in bed. Unable to shake the jet lag when Saturday morning came around, she'd slept most of the day, which ultimately made it even worse Saturday night. Luckily, Emily and Jason had been at the ready with films and pizza. They stayed up until the early hours of Sunday morning polishing off the two bottles of gin she'd purchased from the airport.

Alcohol equals sleep.

Alcohol also equals Ashley not remembering all of the things she'd planned on saying to her ex-fiancée when they met up on Sunday night.

It was Sunday; was she any closer to deciding what she wanted to tell Madison? Absolutely not. The truth would be a good start, but the whole truth and nothing but the truth? She wasn't sure that was an oath she could commit to.

She'd forced herself to wake up at 11:00 a.m. that morning. The room stopped spinning after two aspirin and a large fry-up. She'd never been so thankful for Joe's corner shop and his unlimited supply of eggs. The looming hangover and anxiety about returning to work the next day only briefly affected her well-being. The thought of talking to Madison that night at precisely 7:00 p.m. caused her much greater concern.

As helpful as Jason and Emily had been—Jason more so. She knew it was a conversation she would have to feel out on her own.

How would she feel?

What if she saw her and realised she still loved her?

Did she still love her?

It was likely. Those feelings don't just go away. She wouldn't be made to feel guilty for them. There was no doubt in her mind that she loved Megan, but that didn't instantly take away everything she'd ever felt for Madison. She hoped that seeing Madison would clarify whether the love she thought had turned romantic had been misconstrued all along.

There was no easy way to do it. The longer she waited, the more she would worry. She had to rip the Band-Aid off, whether she liked it or not.

They'd agreed to meet at the apartment—a public place was off the cards. Emily had agreed to vacate. Dinner with Sofia meant she would be occupied for most of the evening. There was nothing left to do but wait. Ashley sat tapping her fingers on the side of the sofa. She sat at the desk in her bedroom reorganising the bits of paperwork she'd already reorganised once before. She moved to the kitchen, and she wiped down the worktops for the third time that day, impatiently flitting from one spot to the next. Time moved slower than when she had to ride in the elevator at work with the weird guy from the eighth floor. It was the most awkward part of her workday whenever it happened. All she needed now was some instrumental music.

What she couldn't understand was her need to light candles, have drinks ready and play low soothing background noise from the vintage record player in the corner. She'd opted for some Aretha Franklin, a classic without any personal significance to their relationship. Why do people insist on creating an aura for such a conversation? She wondered. You set the scene for a first date or an engagement when you're at your happiest, but you also set the scene for a breakup? Ashley felt the full circle moment manifesting before her.

The knock on the door made the hairs on her arms stand on end. Her throat tightened. Her heart felt as though it could beat through her chest if it tried. All she needed now was a green mask to resemble Jim Carrey's most iconic role.

One deep breath. Two. Three. Four.

Open the door you idiot, she screamed internally.

"Hi."

"Hey, Ash."

She stood to one side, allowing Madison to brush past; her scent lingered. She wanted to tell her she looked nice, but that felt inappropriate. She wanted to ask her how she'd been, that felt obvious and also inappropriate. She opted for an easy question.

"Do you want a drink?"

"That would be nice. Thank you."

"Coffee?"

"Sure."

It felt strange to Ashley, watching Madison navigate their apartment like a guest. She was so used to seeing her walk across the wooden floor barefoot in a baggy t-shirt with her toothbrush hanging from her mouth; it felt like someone else's memory now.

"There must have been a lot going on at work?"

"Huh?"

"Emily said how busy you'd been when I spoke to her last."

"Oh yeah, you know what it gets like."

"I'm glad actually; I thought you'd fled the country and not told me." Madison laughed, trying to ease the tension. Ashley cringed. *Now's your opportunity,* she thought.

"I just had a lot of deadlines to meet with the column, that's all."

Wimp.

"How's that going?"

"Really good actually. I now report directly to Sonia every Monday. We agree on what stories to run with, and I do the research. I love it."

"Good, I'm happy for you." Ashley handed her a mug with the letter M on it—not on purpose. "Thank you."

She took one sip. "I can't lie to you; I have missed these coffees."

"I can't take all the credit; the machine does the majority of the work." They laughed.

They took seats at opposite ends of the sofa. Ashley angled her body towards Madison, mindful of seeming too closed off. The distance between them felt abnormal.

"So . . ." Ashley said.

"I guess I should tell you why I wanted to see you." Madison inhaled. "I've been thinking a lot lately about our wedding day. About how I handled the situation. If I was too quick to abandon us. It was hard for me to hear Megan say the things she did. It clarified a lot for me. What I regret is not allowing you the chance to explain yourself. I jumped to the worst possible conclusion, and I just assumed you felt the same way without giving you the chance to tell me otherwise."

Ashley's gulp was audible. "Okay . . ."

"I have missed you so much this past month. It's hard losing someone you love. You were my best friend and my love; that's made this even harder." Madison's eyes glazed over. "I feel lost without you. I tried to hate you at first. I tried to paint this picture in my mind that you were some heartless person who'd been fooling around with Megan behind my back for months. That worked for a week, but deep down I knew that wasn't you. When I couldn't force myself to hate you anymore, I began to miss you."

Ashley stared at the coffee mug, watching the froth slowly manoeuvre its way around the rim. She'd never stared so intently at a cup before. It was as though it would give her some answers.

Why couldn't you have said these things three weeks ago? That's what she wanted to say. Then again, would it have mattered? Now she'd finally opened her eyes to the truth. She suspected eventually she would've found her way to Megan.

"I miss you too."

The words were sincere; she didn't have to force them. She did miss Madison, but probably not in the way that Madison missed her. Ashley didn't miss the intimacy. She missed her best friend. She missed the girl who used to get home blind-drunk at 4:00 a.m. and eat pickles, the teenage girl who used to cut out the faces of all the "hot" famous people and write about each of them in her journal. She missed the girl who could make her laugh uncontrollably whenever she was in a bad mood by making animal noises and twerking. That was her best friend, the girl she'd known pretty much her whole life.

"But . . ." Madison reached out and touched her leg. "Ash . . . look at me."

"There is no but."

"Then why did I envision your reaction differently?"

"I do love you Mads . . ." Ashley paused. *Just tell her.*

"But . . ."

The hope slowly drained from her eyes. "The time apart, it's given me time to think as well. I think we might have rushed into getting married."

"Oh." Madison placed her coffee on the table.

"This isn't easy for me to say. I waited by the phone in the days after the wedding, waiting desperately for you to say something like this." That part was the truth.

"What changed?"

Megan, the word bounced around her head like a ping pong ball. *Megan, Megan, Megan.* She couldn't bring herself to say her name out loud.

"Time." Ashley reached for Madison's hand. "I love you. That will never change."

"You're just not in love with me."

The silence was enough to foretell her response.

"I'm sorry, Mads."

"This isn't what I expected. You begged me to stay. What if I had? Would you have had this epiphany a month later?"

"I don't know."

Madison snatched her hand away from Ashley's grasp. "I should have known. I had reservations about this, about us. Now I have lost the person who was going to be my wife and my best friend. For what?" Madison stood up and stormed towards the door. "Is it Megan?"

"No." *Idiot. Lying will get you nowhere.*

"So, what now?"

"You don't have to lose me. We have been best friends for longer than I can remember. I want you in my life." Ashley walked towards her. "I need you in my life."

"I don't know if I can do that. I need some time."

"Take as long as you need. I don't want you walking away from here thinking I don't want you in my life."

Madison sighed. "Do you really think we can go back to that? I'm looking at you right now and I want to kiss you. What if that doesn't go away?" She sniffled, grabbed her jacket and forcefully dragged the zip up towards her neck.

Please don't kiss me, Ashley thought. That was not something she wanted to explain to Megan.

"It might not be easy, but I'm willing to try, if you are."

"I can't promise anything right now." She kissed Ashley on the cheek, lingering for a moment. "I love you."

Just like that the door fell back on its hinges and she was gone.

How the hell did I get into this position? Ashley contemplated. With every blessing came complications. She wrote about people day in day out who were unlucky in love. She hadn't really been able to sympathise because she was fortunate enough to be loved by two women. Two women who she couldn't fault, two women who would be evenly matched in their comparable pros and cons, but like Ross in *Friends,* there was only one real con on Madison's list. *She wasn't Megan.*

5

Ashley

The next morning Ashley arrived at work without really understanding how she'd arrived. There was a train involved, she knew that much, but her mind was so pre-occupied she didn't recall the journey. Normally, someone's suffocating body odour or inability to talk at a normal human pitch would stick with her—the joys of commuting.

That morning—nothing.

Now, she sat at her desk overwhelmed by the number of meetings she had to attend and the lack of time to digest the night before. Maybe that was a good thing.

The statistics from her column highlighted its success. An email from Sonia praised her for writing such relatable stories, but it made her expectations very clear. She wanted the following month's schedule on her desk by 5:00 p.m.

Impossible?

Almost, but in the publishing world, deadlines were put in place to be beaten. Dedicating the time to write stories in England had proven difficult with such a welcome distraction, but she'd managed to write three weeks' worth of stories. Whilst she was there, numerous emails from people across the country arrived into her inbox. There were almost too many to handle.

She had the material; she just needed the days to be able to put the words into *Time's* worthy articles.

She'd written several personal articles after Sonia had prompted her to use her own experiences in her work. Her current romantic troubles would make for great reading, but she didn't want to publish them. The idea of thousands of people knowing her best-friend had confessed her love for her on the day of her wedding, which resulted in a runaway bride scenario, and then Ashley realising she actually loved her best-friend back; it was too complicated, and too intrusive. It was still so fresh. Then there was the teeny tiny minor detail that she'd yet to tell Madison about Megan.

She had such articles for back up, at least for now, but Sonia's mood dictated what got published, and she hoped the public's stories would suffice.

She'd spent a full day in England siphoning out the best of the hundreds of emails. She'd reached out for more information from the ones that stood out, and she'd hit send on the generic—*Thank you. Unfortunately, your story isn't what we're looking for at this time*—message.

Janine (48) claimed she desperately wanted to reconnect with the love of her life after a whirlwind date at a concert. The story seemed intriguing until further down she said the young man was of celebrity status and had a chequered past. She didn't want to name names, but there was a large store on Broadway that sold tiny little coloured chocolates whose name just happened to sound like his. It took a second, but once it clicked, it wasn't something she was about to get into. A rapper's groupie in the early '00s was way out of Ashley's comfort zone.

Hannah (29) met someone special online whilst playing *Grand Theft Auto*. The two hit it off and continued meeting every day for months until things started getting competitive. She beat him at several video games and he stopped showing up online. *Sore loser* had been Ashley's only thought. Why she wanted to find him made no sense. The requests had been quirky, random, completely unfeasible and eventually romantic.

"Welcome back, Ashley." The voice made her jump. She was buried in her next lot of emails. The office was loud, but over time Ashley had learnt to tune out all but the important sounds, like Sonia's heels clicking along the floor and the vacant sound of the coffee machine.

"Thanks, Carly." She sat at the desk next to hers. They conversed once or twice a day, normally about the latest news scandal, but their jobs were different. Carly worked on digital ads and marketing; it was a subject Ashley knew little about.

"I see the column is doing great. Sonia asked me to work on an advertising campaign for next month. Do you want to see?"

"Sure, that'd be amazing."

Carly began clicking wildly from one screen to the next showing Ashley her initial ideas.

"I compiled a report for last month. I want to focus on the viewability for readers. The majority of traffic comes through the app. I want to make sure your column is as accessible and user friendly as possible through that platform in particular. I made three custom wraps to choose from. Do you like it so far?"

"I love it. Seriously, you've done an amazing job. When does Sonia sign off on this?"

"Friday. Although, my aim is to get it to her by Wednesday. You know what she's like."

Everyone knew Sonia's expectations. The first thing she said to her new hires was, "If I set a deadline, beat it. If I want it for Monday afternoon, I really want it for Monday morning. Always aim to be two steps ahead of the competition." The advice stuck.

"Yes, I do." Ashley's phone buzzed; she saw Megan's name appear. "I need to take this. I'll be back." She made a beeline for the coffee machine, trying to hide her obvious grin.

"Hey."

"Hi, I miss you," Megan said.

Ashley chuckled. "I miss you too. Is that why you're calling?"

"Pretty much. I didn't get to speak with you last night, and I just wanted to check that everything went okay."

The time difference whilst Megan was in England meant they didn't speak as often as Ashley would like.

"It went as well as it could go."

"Did she want to get back together?"

"I think that was implied." Ashley placed the disposable cup on the surface intended and pressed Americano.

"How do you feel about that?"

"Obviously, it would have been easier if she didn't want that, but I tried to be as honest with her as I could without hurting her feelings. I told her I still wanted her in my life, at some point. Even if that's months or years down the line, it doesn't matter."

"Do you think you can be friends again?"

She heard the click of the break room door, and in walked Jeff the maintenance guy. "Yes. I think our friendship is strong enough to get through it. At least, I hope it is. Obviously, that would have to be okay with you." She removed her cup from the coffee machine and headed for the door. She got an eyeful of Jeff's exposed backside on the way out. *Eww.*

"I'll support whatever you want to do."

"Thank you."

Ashley reached her desk and set the coffee cup on the table.

"Should I be expecting some hate mail this week?" Megan jested.

"What do you mean?" Ashley asked.

"I can't imagine she was pleased when you told her about us."

Silence. Panic.

"Shit," Ashley whispered.

"Ash?"

"I . . . didn't . . . exactly . . . tell her."

"What do you mean?"

She looked around for witnesses to the conversation before covering her mouth. "I didn't know how."

"Didn't know how, or didn't want to?" Megan questioned sharply.

Ashley gulped. "Both. I knew it would break her heart. I didn't want to be cruel."

"You don't have to be cruel, Ash. You just need to tell the truth. What if she thinks there's still a chance the two of you could get back together?"

"She doesn't."

"How do you know?"

"Does it matter? I want to be with you." Ashley tried to divert the topic of conversation from Madison's feelings onto her own.

Megan sighed. "Do you?"

"That's unfair. You know I do."

Ashley heard what sounded like a wardrobe door slam in the background. "I need to go. I told my dad I'd play two on two with him and a couple of his work friends."

"Can we talk about this later?"

"I don't know if I'll be awake when you finish work." She was being stubborn. Granted, it would be close to midnight in England by the time Ashley arrived home, but that had never been a problem before.

"Can you try? I feel like you're upset, and I want to talk about it."

Megan sighed. "Just text me when you're nearly finished."

"Okay."

"Try not to give Madison any more false hope between now and tonight will you."

"Ouch." Maybe she deserved that.

The phone line went dead. How was she the bad person? Not only in the eyes of Madison, but Megan too. She flopped back into her chair. *Maybe it will blow over by tonight*, she hoped.

The target on her back was growing. She wasn't about to forget Julie and Nancy either. Ashley had some apologising to do regarding the catering money Julie had forked out for the wedding. There hadn't been a—*return on the day for a full refund if the bride does a runner*—policy. Nancy had paid for her suit, which hadn't gone to waste. Technically she'd worn it. There were some photos taken in said suit, and if she wanted to be really picky, she could wear the suit again, maybe to someone else's wedding. Although, some might think that bad luck, so maybe not to a wedding. Other than a brief—*I'm sorry*—in the days after the wedding,

Ashley had avoided grand apologies. She felt so much shame that evading the situation seemed like the better option.

Dwelling on her personal relationships wasn't going to get her through the mound of paperwork and emails that read *URGENT* in the subject line of her inbox, so she reluctantly put her phone on *do not disturb* and turned her attention back to her computer. She had a long day ahead.

***

The journey home made her contemplate why she didn't hail a cab more often. The subway was cheap, it was quick and it did what it was designed to do, but it often felt like she was stepping into another world when she left the open air behind. She came across an older gentleman who went out of his way to sit beside her. He reeled off all the things he hated about the subway and the Bronx, seemingly where he'd grown up. Ashley ignored the occasional huff as she flicked the pages of the book she was reading. This behaviour eventually prompted him to stop talking.

The commute home took twelve minutes, give or take a minute, it wasn't enough time to really settle into a book, but she felt it a necessary companion to avoid such conversations—it didn't always work.

Jane Eyre, the Charlotte Brontë classic, was her latest book of choice. She'd read it once or twice before, but she found with the nineteenth century novels it took three or four reads to understand the depth of what was happening.

To her displeasure, the book of choice often became a topic of conversation. A woman to her right lingered, shuffling her feet, crossing and un-crossing her arms until she finally said, "*Jane Eyre*—That's one of my favourites. It's a real quest for equality and independence don't you think?"

The conversation could go one of two ways. If Ashley responds, agreeing with the random commuter, said commuter will take it as an invitation to reel off Charlotte Brontë's collection like she's some time-travelling, nineteenth century reincarnation. Or she opts for the response, "I'm unsure, it's my first time reading it," prompting the woman to turn to her left primed and ready to bother the poor kid with headphones on. Like Ashley he is just trying to ride the subway in peace. Ashley opted for the latter.

Peace however was a luxury, with two minutes left of her journey an angry woman began screaming at the top of her voice, "I'll kill her." It was unclear whom she was referring to, or whether the woman referred to was onboard the C train. Either way everyone got an earful of shrieked obscenities as she made her way up the car.

Don't make eye contact with her for God's sake. In times like this, whichever book she'd chosen became her saving grace.

Thankfully, she got off the subway alive, and made a beeline for the exit to the street. As soon as she reached ground level her phone rang.

"Oh, thank God."

"Hey girl, everything okay?" Jason greeted her.

"I just had the subway ride from hell. Why can't people just leave me alone?"

"Tell me about it. I refuse to ride that disease ridden metal tin any longer. Since my experience last year, I would rather pay $150 a week in taxi fares."

"Ah yes, we don't need to get into that."

Jason's dramatic encounters were often amusing, but a topic to avoid.

"Very true. Anyway, the reason I'm calling is about my birthday. You know it's this Saturday?"

"How could I forget. Have you decided on the venue?" She stopped at the street vendor outside the station where she purchased a giant bag of potato chips and a candy bar.

"Well, this is the thing. The owner of my bar said I can have the VIP area if I want it. Obviously, some free drinks would be a given, so with my current cash flow constraints it seems like the healthier option."

She didn't wait to rip open the candy bar. "As opposed to hiring out the suite at the Four Seasons? Yeah, I'd say that's certainly healthier on your bank balance."

"Exactly, now that I'm saving to get my own place, I need to behave myself."

Ashley chuckled. At least three times a year Jason would say he needed to start saving; it never happened.

"Does that mean you're returning the Prada bag you purchased last week?"

"That was a birthday gift, and besides, I said I *need* to behave myself. I never said that would always be possible."

"Right, okay." She dodged a kid on a skateboard whilst maintaining a firm grip on the bag of chips under her arm.

"Back to the bar, do you think that's a good idea?" Ashley never understood Jason's need for reassurance because he would always do exactly what he wanted regardless, but she played along anyway.

"Sure, it'll be perfect."

"Will Megan be back in the country by then?" He enquired reluctantly.

"Yes, she flies back on Friday." Ashley was counting down the minutes.

"Hmm."

"What?"

"Well . . . that was the other thing."

She crunched with meaning on the last section of the candy bar. The dryness of the peanut butter sticking to the roof of her mouth caused her words to come out stifled, "Spit it out Jason."

"Normally, you, Em, and Madison plan something for my birthday. Obviously this year is different, but it's always been our thing. . ."

"I'm sorry. . . I did offer. . ."

Jason cut her off. "No, I don't mean that. I wanted to plan it myself. I guess what I'm saying is I couldn't not invite Madison to my party. Which leaves me in a difficult spot because she doesn't know about you and Megan which kind of puts me in the middle."

"Oh . . ." The thought of Madison and Megan in the same room gave Ashley heart palpations. It was too soon. "Maybe Madison won't come?"

"She RSVP'd this morning."

"Ah, right. So, you're basically saying only one of them can come, and that one is Madison?"

"The alternative, you tell Madison you're dating Megan. Then I'm positive she won't come."

"I'm not ready for that."

Jason sniggered. "I didn't think so."

Ashley waved at Howard in his bagel truck before hopping up the steps towards her apartment. "So, there's no way they can both come?" She already knew the answer.

"There is one way."

"Yeah?" Optimism.

"You can pretend you're Rachael in that *Friends* episode we love where she has to keep her parents apart. We can put Megan in the VIP area, Madison in the restroom and you can just run between the two."

Ashley rolled her eyes. "You're an idiot. I thought you had a genuine suggestion." She sighed. "My head hurts. I've had a long day, and this is not helping."

"You could invite her, but you'd have to avoid looking like a couple. Maybe speak to Megan. I don't care either way. If there's tequila, naked men and gifts then I'm happy. Minimal drama I can deal with. My life is one big drama, so it's nothing new."

"All I took from that was naked men. Why are there going to be naked men?"

"I was hoping you'd get me a stripper."

"You . . ." Ashley dropped her keys as she fumbled to get inside. "Shit . . . hold on . . ." Once inside she threw the chips on the counter. "Sorry, you never asked for a stripper?"

"I'm a gay man who loves nothing more than rubbing oil on chiselled bodies. I have a membership card to Hunk-O-Mania for a reason."

"Jesus. Okay. I'll see what I can do."

"Mom, you can't say that," Jason bellowed. "Honey, I gotta go, my mom is watching the new season of *RuPaul* and I need to correct her pronouns."

"Okay, I'll call you tomorrow about Saturday."

"Got it. Be bold, sexy and powerful. Bye."

Like clockwork, just as her phone call with Jason ended, Megan's name appeared on her phone screen.

There was no easy way to tell the girl you're newly dating that she can't come to your best friend's party because your ex-fiancée will be there.

"I hate my life," Ashley muttered.

6

Megan

Drills. Drills. Drills.

The only way to develop muscle memory and good habits is by practicing consistently. Megan was used to concentrating with unreal effectiveness and making sure she had the right form. First and foremost she was used to drill after drill. Growing up she was drilled to know where to stand, how to stand, when to release, when to spin, when to drop her shoulder and how to dribble. The list of drills was endless.

There was a drill for every single move and technique. When she witnessed the Kobe Bryant fadeaway for the first time, she went out to the court and tried the same move one hundred times. The frustration at not being able to make the shot only spurred her on. Every single day she practiced the same shot exactly one hundred times. One year later she'd mastered one of the most indefensible and deadly shots in the game of basketball—almost to perfection.

As she grew older, she'd had to adjust her technique. Just because she consistently hit the shot 90% of the time didn't mean she would forever hit that shot. The competition became fierce. In high school she came up against six-foot defenders for the first time. She came up against coaches who'd watched her game and knew her offensive moves better than they knew their own. By the time she arrived at Stanford her fatal fadeaway was more of a harmless jump shot. That frustrated her; from then on she returned to her one hundred shots a day. Often, she would request the services of another team member, they added the pressure, giving a normal practice that game day feeling.

The clouds gathered above what was left of the blue sky, darkening into a stormy grey. The first splatter of rain hit her forehead as she spun, leapt and released the ball for the eighty-seventh time. Watching the ball glide through the air was her favourite part; it felt like a slow-motion montage. As her feet hit the floor, she observed the ball drop through the net. Thirteen more attempts and she moved on to high-speed shooting drills. The rain poured as she ran from half-court to the top of the key at full speed. The ability to shoot whilst on the run was another skill she'd tried to master. The stop-and-pop was a necessary weapon in her arsenal.

The ball slipped from her grip. The slight fumble caused her upward motion to lose rhythm, and threw the trajectory of the ball off course. It fell short of the rim entirely.

"Ahhh. Come on."

She picked up the loose ball and backpedalled to the half-court line. This time she tried a simple one dribble pull up. She made eight of her first ten shots despite the downpour. When she got to shot number sixteen her legs refused to give her the lift she needed; her consistent stroke failed. That was the barrier she had to break through. The fourth quarter intensity was like nothing else. When everyone was exhausted and fighting for every last possession, perfecting drills gave her the upper hand. They allowed her to be the difference, the game-changer.

She found the strength to quicken her pace. The puddles forming beneath her feet splashed with each stomp towards the top of the key. It was impossible to tell which beads of water dripping from her face were perspiration and which were rain. It didn't matter; the combination soaked her jersey. She only realised the rain was cold when she came to a halt after twenty shots and bent over sapped of energy.

Basketball was Megan's escape; it always had been. It was her distraction from real world elements set to cause worry and doubt. As soon as the ball stopped bouncing, the uneasiness returned drowning out any positive thoughts in her mind like the water drowned her now skintight clothing.

She heard footsteps to her right; they quickened, the splash of water making their presence known. Her dad barrelled past her pulling the basketball skilfully from the ground. He headed straight for a wide-open one-handed dunk.

"Your dad's still got it."

She laughed at his outlandish celebration. "Anyone would think you're Kobe."

"I told you about the time I met Kobe, didn't I?"

"Yes Dad, once or twice." She finally stood up straight, her breathing back to a somewhat normal rhythm.

"Are you okay, kiddo?"

"Yeah."

"Are you sure? Because I watched you from the window. You never play with that kind of intensity unless your mid-season or you're angry."

"I'm not angry." She sounded angry.

"Then what? Upset? Annoyed?"

"Why do I need to be upset or annoyed?"

"You're out here running drills in the pouring rain." He raised his eyebrow.

"I love the rain."

"Now I know you're lying." He reached forwards and lovingly brushed the hair from her eyes. "Come on, kiddo, you know you can tell me anything."

She loved her dad more than she could put into words. Their bond was special. They shared the same passion and drive in life. They were the same person, or cut from the same basketball themed cloth. That's what her mom always said.

"I'm scared," she admitted.

"What's scaring you?"

She sighed. "Can I ask you something?" He nodded; the rain slowed to a light drizzle. "How did you know mom was the one?"

"I didn't. Not right away. I told you how I'd asked her out on multiple occasions, but she was seeing some guy that looked like Tupac." He rolled his eyes comically. "How was I supposed to compete with some guy who wore tight tank tops, always had the freshest haircut, and had the kind of voice that sounded like Martin Luther King reincarnated. I was a skinny white kid from North Carolina." Michael laughed.

"I have seen pictures of you when you were younger, and I can't disagree."

"I was thankful for him though; he was the reason I started hitting the gym. Fast forward two years and I had the muscles to match my lanky frame." Michael flexed, and Megan cringed.

"Every cloud."

"Exactly. If I'd have stayed that skinny, would I have been as effective in my basketball career? Maybe not, so there are positives in every situation." Michael dribbled the ball between his legs, his handles were still top-notch. "Your mother was a picture of perfection. I knew I wanted to get to know her the second I laid eyes on her, but she had someone and when she didn't, I did. It took a year or two before we found ourselves single at the same time."

Like me and Ashley, Megan thought.

"There was one time, we'd been together almost two years. I was sat in my dorm angry at myself, at my teammates and my performance overall. We'd just lost the final D1 game of the season; it was a must-win and our ticket to the playoffs. We'd worked so hard all season. I'd given every second of my time to the game, to my team, often going weeks without seeing your mother. The coach would say to us, "Women are a distraction. You've got your whole life to be distracted, so you won't do it on my time." I took on that mentality. I'm surprised your mother stood with me through all the cancelled dates, the last-minute practices, the road trips and team bonding sessions. I was dating the game of basketball, not your mom."

"I'm surprised she didn't kick your ass to the curb." Megan grinned, her mom was fierce. She knew her worth, so the revelation surprised her.

"So am I! I wouldn't have blamed her. After that game I was inconsolable. I'd been horrible to her on the phone, and I was frustrated with everyone and everything. Your mom turned up the next day with my favourite quesadilla in hand and these cookies her mom used to make. She'd asked for the recipe and baked them that morning. She'd spelt out *I love you* with chocolate chips."

"Aww that is literally the cutest thing ever!"

"I know. I wanted to wallow in my own self-pity, but I couldn't be mad at your mom. Her smile instantly made me smile. She started dancing around the room trying her hardest to make me laugh. That's when I knew that I didn't just love her, but she was the one for me. She was it. She did what nobody else had ever been able to do. To this day, she's the only person who can bring me back from rock bottom."

Megan smiled. "That's really sweet, Dad."

"You obviously asked me that for a reason. Are you wondering if Ashley is the one?"

Megan ran her fingers through her hair, wiping raindrops from her forehead.

"Not necessarily, I know it's too soon for any of that. We've only just started dating."

"Yes, but you've loved her for a long time." That was a fact.

"I do love her."

"So why are you scared?"

"What if she's not the one? What if this idea of Ashley being my person turns out to be false? What if we don't make it?"

Michael cradled the ball against his torso, staring intently at his daughter. "Sweetheart, what if you do? Don't get yourself worked up over something that may never happen. Has something made you question the longevity of your relationship?"

The conversation Monday night had thrown her state of bliss into disarray. She was all set to return to New York in two days' time. The sole purpose of returning so early was to spend time with Ashley. She would have stayed in England for most of the off-season were it not for her, but the thought of being away from Ashley for three months was unbearable.

"I just worry that her and Madison have things to figure out. They almost got married for God's sake. Those feelings don't just disappear. What if she changes her mind? She hasn't even told Madison yet, about us. Then there's Jason's party this weekend. I'm not allowed to go. All I want to do is tell the world she's mine. It's all just a big sack of shit." Megan grabbed the ball from her dad's hands, bouncing it aggressively towards the basket for an easy uncontested layup. She missed. In retaliation she slammed the ball into the ground with force watching it launch into the air like a rocket.

"Hey, hey . . . listen to me." Michael said. She turned back to her dad. "Ashley came to the airport at the drop of a hat to be with *you*. She could have stayed in New York. She didn't. These things are complicated. She has to be respectful to Madison. You said yourself she's a nice girl?"

Megan nodded. "She is."

"If Ashley is as kind and considerate as you say she is, she won't want to hurt Madison. I know that's hard for you. You probably feel like the 'other woman', but that's only temporary. Give it time."

"Maybe you're right."

"She loves you, darling. Trust me. How could she not?" He reached for his daughter, pulling her in for a strong embrace. Megan was above average height, at five foot eight. She never felt small unless she was hugging her dad. He had almost a foot on her. She buried her head in his chest. "I love you, Dad."

"I love you too, sweetheart." He looked up at the clouds gathering above. "Now, let's get inside. I'm freezing."

7

Ashley

Jason sprawled across Ashley's bed. His long limbs falling off the sides. It was his idea that they all get ready together, Madison included. She'd politely declined.

Emily was bouncing from one end of the apartment to the other after making margaritas in which the presence of tequila largely overpowered the lime juice. It reminded Ashley of when they'd first started living together; every hour had been cocktail hour. Ashley and Madison's experience in bar work provided the mixologists. Their ability to barter with their boss meant a few extra bottles of their choosing would make their way onto the orders at trade price.

Ashley grabbed a fresh towel from the laundry basket and made her way towards the bathroom.

"Are you only just getting a shower?" Jason sighed.

She pointed towards his casual attire. "You're not even dressed."

"Yes, but I'm showered."

"I know you are. I couldn't get into the bathroom for an hour whilst you did God knows what." Ashley flapped her towel around hysterically.

"Manscaping is a very important part of my routine."

"I swear to God Jason, if the shower is full of your pubic curls, I will shave a giant line through your hair whilst you sleep."

He gasped. "How dare you come for my hair. Do you know how long it took Dr. B to get these waves? And the fade . . ." He pulled a small pocket mirror from his trousers and began to admire himself. "Damn I look good. I don't know another barber who can do a blurry fade like this."

Ashley dropped her head in disbelief. "The fact that you carry a pocket mirror to check yourself out sums you up. Remind me why you call your barber a Dr. again?"

He pursed his lips, wiping at the edges of his hair softly. "Because he surgically removes the hair from my head with the precision of a god."

"Right."

Jason leapt up and grabbed the towel from Ashley's grasp.

"Seriously, Jason? You're such a child." She couldn't help but smirk.

"Yes, I am, but you love me."

He ran towards the living area and began whipping Emily's backside. She pretended to enjoy it and the whole scene made Ashley chuckle. "I can't believe, out of all the people in this world, I ended up with you two idiots as my best friends."

They stopped, completely offended.

"Rude," Emily said.

"But true," Jason added.

"Can I have my towel back, please? You'll be annoyed with me when we're late because I'm still in the shower."

"Sure." He handed it over willingly. "By the way, have you spoken to Megan yet?"

"You mean since you asked me an hour ago? No."

"What are you gonna do?" Emily chipped in.

"I obviously want to see her, but she's still annoyed by the, not being *allowed* to come to the party, situation." She'd had a brief conversation that morning with a jet-lagged Megan. The tone had been hostile.

"I feel partly responsible for that." Jason frowned.

"As much as I'd love to blame you, it's not your fault. I'm the one who nearly married my best friend and two weeks later flew to England with my other best friend who I was blindly in love with."

"True. It is your fault." Jason smirked. "But I have an idea."

"I'm listening."

"Emily will shower Madison with drinks until she's so merry she doesn't care if Megan is there or not. Then you ask Megan to come a little later and we'll figure out the rest from there."

"Wow, that plan sucks!" Emily slurred.

"Sorry, are you drunk?" Jason looked at Emily in disgust.

"No!"

"You sound drunk," Ashley added.

"I bit my tongue earlier, okay? It's swollen." She stormed towards the kitchen and searched for some ice. "Thanks for pointing it out though, now I feel stupid." She launched three separate ice cubes into her mouth one after the other.

"Seriously though, I agree with Em, it's a crappy plan," Ashley said.

"Well, when you come up with a better one you let me know." Jason clicked his fingers and bounced towards the bedroom. "Let's go ladies; it's nearly showtime."

***

Visiting the bar where Jason worked brought back fond memories. Only recently had the significance of those memories come to light. The image of the girl in the tight white dress with flowing brown hair flashed before her eyes. It was a picture engrained on Ashley's mind; despite the five years that had passed she felt right back in that moment whenever she stepped foot in Midtown 101.

What if she'd never met Megan?

What if that night she hadn't had the courage to approach her?

Would fate have brought them together some other way?

The questions all seemed irrelevant, but she did wonder, as she eyed the exact spot where she first laid eyes on Megan. The nostalgia was intense. What she would give to relive that night. To see Megan for the first time again. How different it was now.

Madison stood in the corner of the room, a few steps to the left of where Megan once stood. She wore a figure-hugging black dress, similar in style and shape to the white dress Megan had worn. The difference in the viewing was the pang of guilt in the pit of Ashley's stomach. The feeling was entirely dissimilar to the feelings the night she met Megan. Back then she felt nothing but butterflies and elation. Tonight's guilt came from knowing the choice she'd made would ultimately break Madison's heart.

It was torture to finally acknowledge her love for Megan after so many years only to keep it contained. It was the right thing to do, she knew that deep down, but it didn't make it any easier. She loved Megan; she'd always loved Megan. That in itself was a revelation for the ages. Waiting for Jason's birthday to tell Madison the truth was unkind. She didn't want to make the night about her, but how much longer could she go on hiding it? She didn't have to tell her, the peer pressure caused her so much anxiety she'd been unable to sleep the night before. Ashley had to come clean, but watching Madison smile, and laugh so freely caused her stomach to churn. She wiped at her forehead. *Is it hot in here?*

Ashley had called Megan an hour earlier asking her to come, but the choice was hers. Megan made it clear she would prefer to avoid the situation. Ashley was disappointed that she'd have to wait even longer to see her, but she felt relief that there would be no uncomfortable encounter with Madison.

"Are you going to talk to her?" Emily leant over the back of the chair, yelling above the music. Diana Ross's "I'm Coming Out" had the speakers vibrating and Jason whipping his head around like he'd been possessed by the air dancer from the local car lot.

"I said 'Hello' when I came in."

Emily sighed. "Just go over and talk to her. She already feels like she can't come over to this side of the room because you might suddenly combust."

"What are you talking about? Why would I comb dust?"

"I said COMBUST!" Emily yelled. The music cut and switched to the next track just as she yelled. Ashley almost fell off her chair in a fit of laughter. "I hate you."

"It's that fat tongue!" she mimicked Emily.

"Stop making me yell when my mouth hurts." She reached for her tongue, pulling it to the side to show Ashley the red pulsating lump.

"You bit your tongue; you didn't have it surgically removed. Stop being dramatic."

"You know how much effort it takes to bite those sweets! I'm surprised I've not completely severed it."

Ashley rolled her eyes. "I'm going over." There was no time like the present.

Madison smiled in her direction as she approached. She went via the bar, throwing back a shot for courage and collecting a margarita as her peace offering. Ashley felt eyes on her. She knew Jason would be watching intently, Emily too.

The gap between them closed to within touching distance. The music lowered at the same moment that she reached her arm out and said, "Drink?"

"Thank you. You didn't have to do that."

Ashley raised her eyebrow, as if to say, *it's the least I could do.*

"I noticed you were running low."

"Observant of you." Madison smirked. "I thought you were going to avoid me all night," she joked. She was in a pleasant mood; maybe it was the alcohol.

"Yeah, sorry," Ashley said.

"I understand. It's weird, isn't it?"

"A little," Ashley agreed.

"I'm surprised Megan's not here?"

That didn't take long, Ashley thought. "We didn't think it would be appropriate."

"We?"

"Me and Jason."

"Ah okay." Madison took a sip of her drink; the salt caused her lips to curl. "I love these things, but I don't think I'll ever get used to that sour taste." She waited. Ashley wasn't sure if she was expecting her to fill the silence. What was she supposed to say? A few seconds felt like a minute. Then Madison said something she wasn't expecting.

"Did you enjoy your time in England?"

Gulp. Ashley stiffened instantly.

She shifted her weight, fidgeting noticeably with the glass at her fingertips. It didn't take a genius to see how uncomfortable she felt. *How the hell does she know?* She thought. There was no denying it now, she wanted to say "England?" as though she had no idea what she was referring to, but Madison wasn't bluffing, and Ashley owed her more respect than that.

"Who told you?"

"Your email account was still logged in on my laptop."

Shit. Damn autosave.

"Oh." She cursed herself internally for all the times she'd left her laptop at work and had to use Madison's. *So stupid.*

"I was going to tell you."

"Really? When?" Madison's stare turned icy.

Ashley cleared her throat; the ability to breathe became a problem.

"Yes." There was no conviction in her response. "I wanted too, several times, I just didn't know how to say it."

"So, what? You just lied to my face instead?"

"I'm sorry." Ashley rubbed at her jaw, her head was throbbing.

"For which part? Lying to me or replacing me weeks after our wedding day?" Madison scowled.

"I didn't replace you." Ashley frowned.

"So, you're not seeing Megan?"

Her muscles tightened, and the palms of her hands felt damp. *You already know?* There was no use in lying anymore.

"Our situation has changed, yes." Ashley's gaze fell to the floor. She braced herself for the contents of Madison's drink to end up all over her face, or worse for the whole bar to turn into a documentary she'd seen on National Geographic, tables flipping, glasses smashing and Madison hunting her like a lion from the Serengeti.

Madison laughed sarcastically. "Of course it has."

"I. . . didn't plan it. . . it just sort of happened."

"You didn't plan to what? Fall into bed with Megan? So, you just went to England, and happened to bump into her then? How coincidental." She scoffed. "I actually can't fucking believe you."

"I never wanted to hurt you."

"Oh, give me a break, Ashley. You only thought about yourself."

"That's not true. Your feelings are all I have thought about."

"Did you think about my feelings when you were half way around the world, cuddled up in bed with *her*, and lying to me?" Madison slammed her empty drink down on the table. "You even had Emily lie for you!"

Madison threw her hands up. "I need a minute." She joined the queue at the bar. Ashley didn't move, she was frozen to the spot.

How did I end up in this situation?

Jason was oblivious to their conversation, which she was thankful for. She watched him prance around the dance floor, he was in his element as the centre of attention.

Madison returned with a glass of wine in hand. She looked more composed. Her flushed cheeks had subsided. The pounding in Ashley's chest began to calm. She'd spent many nights contemplating the very conversation she was having, but nothing prepared her for that moment.

"I never meant to hurt you," Ashley whispered.

"I know." Madison sighed. She stepped a foot closer.

"It was wrong of me to lie, I was just so afraid of losing you."

"No. . . You were being a coward. I know you. You've always been terrible at having difficult conversations."

"That too." Ashley admitted.

"I'm not letting you off the hook here, but I haven't exactly been honest with you or myself either."

Ashley's eyes narrowed. "What do you mean?"

"After our conversation on Sunday. I came to realise that I'd forced myself to believe we were compatible. I confused the love we had for each other as best friends to be something more. That's not to say that I didn't want to marry you, or that I didn't love you. I would have made it work. We had the foundation, but there would have come a time, whether it was one year, two years or ten years down the line when the connection we have as friends wouldn't have been enough. I think that's why you've never been able to fully close the door with Megan."

"Oh." *Is this a trick?*

Madison reached out and placed her hand on Ashley's left arm as she edged closer. "I'm not saying I want to see the two of you together; that would still hurt me." She hesitated. "What I'm saying is, I understand."

"I would never rub that in your face." Ashley said sincerely.

"I should have listened to my intuition." Madison shrugged. "I knew deep down something wasn't right with us, it was just hard to accept, because you know me better than anyone."

"Ditto." Ashley smiled.

"I worry that I won't find someone else who accepts me for me and who ticks my long list of boxes." Madison jested. They both laughed.

The joke eased the tension in Ashley's shoulders, she looked up, and was able to make solid eye contact. "I think you'll be absolutely fine." Ashley smiled softly. There was still one question she desperately wanted the answer to.

"What does this mean for us?"

"I hope we can be friends again one day," Madison said.

All apprehension disappeared; people say time is a healer, and Ashley believed that. The bond they shared had been present since kindergarten. They'd been through bullying, death, divorce, heartbreak, illness and so much more. Together, side by side, they were each other's support systems. Maybe they'd never get back the kind of friendship they once had, but Ashley hoped that in time they could be a shadow of their former selves.

"I'd like nothing more."

Madison leant forwards and kissed Ashley on the cheek; it was a welcome gesture. "I want you to be happy, Ash." As she pulled back, she jabbed Ashley's stomach playfully. "Now I think the least you could do is get me another drink."

"I'll buy you two." She grinned.

***

The next morning a crash jolted Ashley upright from her sleeping position. It was followed by a scream and lots of cursing. Ashley felt surprisingly upbeat despite having drunk enough to kill a small herd of elephants the previous night. When she opened her bedroom door, Emily sat on the floor leaning against the wall. She was cradling her left foot like someone seriously considering their life choices.

"Are you all right?" Ashley asked. The console table that came with the apartment sat in the corridor between their rooms. They'd moved it into every possible position around the apartment, considered taking it to a charity shop, almost sold it, left it outside for someone to take and up cycled it three times before deciding it'd been through too much to give it away.

"Do I look okay? I think I've broken my toe. That table needs to go." She kicked out sharply with her good foot.

"Does it? Or do you need to be more careful? You've stubbed your toe on that table at least five times this year."

Ashley laughed whilst Emily rubbed ferociously at the injured area.

"I swear it moves. In the middle of the night it moves, or it grows or something. It's determined to hurt me."

"Come on. Get up." Ashley held out her hand dragging Emily to her feet. "How're you feeling?"

"Okay." Emily reached the kitchen, pulled a green Gatorade from the fridge and some aspirin off the counter.

"Are you still drunk?"

"Obviously." She nodded vigorously. "You can't wake up hungover if you're still drunk."

The mind of Emily Baker—she always liked to be off the beaten path.

"Eventually you have to wake up sober; you know that, right?"

"Tell that to my mom." Emily replied.

Ashley tapped at her phone; the screen lit up, no messages. She grabbed a large glass of water and retreated to the sofa. Her eyes were still half-closed. She hadn't been prepared for the sun to burn a hole through the blinds the way it did.

She tapped her phone again, still no message.

"Okay, what's going on?" Emily chirped. Ashley stared blankly in her direction. "You've clicked on your phone five times already."

Ashley pushed the phone down the edge of the sofa. Better not to look at it, she thought. "Megan hasn't replied."

"Since last night?" Emily asked.

"Yeah. I thought maybe she'd gone to bed, but still no reply this morning."

"Maybe she's jet-lagged and she's just catching up on her sleep."

Ashley shook her head. "There's no way she would've slept for thirteen hours. She's an early bird; she never sleeps past 8:00 a.m. Something is wrong."

In the pit of her stomach, she knew. Her intuition was telling her something with a mixture of fear, anxiety and concern. Five text messages and two phone calls had gone unanswered. There was no conscious reasoning behind her worry, but when people say, "you just know," well, she did.

"Have you called her this morning?"

"Not yet."

"Then call her," Emily prompted.

Ashley removed her phone from the crease in the sofa and hit the top number on her *most recent call list.* Voicemail.

"Her phones off."

"Okay, did you argue last night? Does she have any reason to not want to speak to you?"

Ashley shook her head. "We didn't argue; if anything she understood why I had my reservations about telling Madison."

"Did you tell her Madison had figured it out?"

"Yes. That was the first message she didn't respond to, which I thought was weird."

"Huh." Emily scratched at her head. "Well, I'm sure there's a perfectly reasonable explanation. Maybe just give her a few hours to see if she responds."

Ashley felt a certain unparalleled feeling of fear. The unpleasant emotion caused by thoughts of the unknown sparked memories from her childhood.

When Ashley was eight years old she lost her mom at a flea market. While looking for her, she spun aimlessly from left to right ducking and diving through a crowd of figures that towered over her. She panicked. She felt afraid. *What if she never found her mom again? What if someone kidnapped her?* Logically, she knew the chances of either of those things happening were slim, but that didn't matter in the moment.

She remembered a vacation in Egypt with her parents; she'd been thirteen. They'd decided to go out for lunch. She hadn't wanted to go. The latest instalment of the *Harry Potter* series had captivated her entire being from the second she'd purchased the book at the airport. If it didn't involve wands or wizardry she simply wasn't interested. After they'd been gone for two hours she became increasingly concerned about their whereabouts. They'd specifically said, "We won't be long." Three hours passed, and there was still no word. She didn't have a mobile phone, so she had no way of contacting them. The sky grew darker as the panic set in. She walked back and forth towards the balcony, pacing the room, increasingly concerned for their safety. *What if her parents had been in an accident? What if they didn't come back for her?* They turned up three and a half hours later with boozy breath and a terrible excuse about bumping into an Egyptian man with curly hair that offered them two for one cocktails.

She remembered the relief that washed over her like it was yesterday. There was no better feeling.

Right then she was feeling that same fear, the deeply instinctual intuition she hadn't experienced since she was a teenager.

"I'm calling Nancy."

The phone went to voicemail. Strange, she thought. Nancy's phone was never off.

"I'll try Julie."

"Do you not think you're overreacting?"

"No, something is wrong."

Emily threw her hands up. "Okay."

Ashley walked around the sofa frantically before sitting on the edge of the matching armchair.

She dialled Julie. Voicemail.

"Okay, what the actual fuck?" She slammed her phone on the coffee table. "That's weird, right?"

"I have to admit that's strange," Emily agreed. "Unless her whole family's been abducted by E.T. there is absolutely no reason all of them would be uncontactable."

Emily drank the remainder of her Gatorade. "Unless . . ."

"What?"

"Nothing." She sat quietly, shrinking back in her seat.

"Em, what?"

"There is one other place I know of where the phone signal is terrible, and they often get asked to switch them off."

Suddenly it dawned on her.

"The emergency room."

8

Ashley

Time stood still.

The earth would never cease to rotate, constantly spinning on its axis, the rotation unnoticeable to Ashley, but in that moment she felt the room spin. It felt eerily quiet; she could see Emily beside her, yet she was numb to her touch. The sound of the TV in the background sounded muffled; she couldn't make sense of the words. A sharp ringing in her ears increased. She wanted to get up, but her body was rooted firmly to the floor. She'd never felt her knees give way before. All her defences were destroyed in an instant leaving her reeling in shock.

Emily's voice broke through in sections. She heard the words but struggled to respond. "Ash . . . Ash . . . can you hear me?" It felt like a dream, one she desperately wanted to wake from. The words were barely above a whisper.

Emily's hand reached for hers. "Ash . . . please talk to me . . . what did she say?"

She turned towards her best friend, mouth open, eyes vacant but no words. "Ashley Stewart, pull yourself together. What did Nancy say?"

Emily's calm, soothing demeanour reverted to her usual no-bullshit attitude which was exactly what Ashley needed.

Nancy. The call. *Oh God.*

"Am I dreaming?"

"No, you're right here with me."

Ashley held out her hands; the shaking reduced to a light tremor. She could hear Emily clearly now. "Ash, what did Nancy say?"

The phone call from Nancy came ten minutes after she'd failed to reach her. The initial relief when her name appeared turned to shear disbelief when she told her the news. Only one part echoed in her mind—*Megan's been in an accident*—Nancy could barely speak which led her to immediately fear the worst.

"Megan's in the hospital," the words leaked from Ashley's parted lips.

"What happened?"

"A car. She's been hit by a car," Ashley murmured.

"Where is she?"

"Lenox Hill."

"Well, let's go. What are you waiting for?" Emily the drill Sergeant reappeared; there was no circumstance she couldn't handle.

Ashley dropped her gaze to the floor. "It's bad, Em."

"Then we need to go and see her, don't we?"

Ashley nodded. "Nancy said she's just got out of surgery." Her eyes welled up. The vacant stare disappeared as the weight of sadness crushed her. "What if she doesn't make it?" Ashley sobbed.

Emily wrapped her arm around Ashley's shoulders. "She will."

They sat that way for over an hour, feeling utterly powerless before Nancy finally confirmed that Megan could have visitors.

***

Outside the hospital, Emily waited. Inside, Ashley asked the receptionist at the main desk to point her towards the ICU. A burst of directions and hand gestures came her way. She got as far as the right turn at the end of the hall before having to revert to following the signs on the wall.

She eventually reached an adult ward, but the signs for the ICU had disappeared. When she returned to the elevator, she observed a woman in a single room. She lay peacefully, her skin fragile and wrinkled, her arms covered in bruises from the constant needles prodding and poking at her frail body. Her wispy grey hair barely covered her head. There was nobody by her side, no husband to hold her hand. Perhaps he had already passed, Ashley thought.

She made a note of the woman's room number; she'd be sure to check back before she left. If she was still alone when Ashley came back, she would sit beside her.

There was nothing to like about hospitals. They are a place you only find yourself when something is wrong. She'd only been twice in her whole life, once for a scan on her stomach when they thought she had gallstones and the second time to visit her great grandmother. Both experiences were horrible. After wandering aimlessly, she asked a member of the staff where to go. They must have sensed her distress because they offered to walk with her.

According to Nancy, Megan was in room 38, the room to the right of the nurse's station. The low lighting throughout the corridors left her with an eerie feeling. The smell of sterilisation filled the air. Doctors and interns rushed from room to room. Ashley feared the unknown as she focused her attention on keeping one foot in front of the other.

When she arrived, the door was ajar; she saw the backs of Nancy and Julie's heads. They stood to the right of the bed, blocking her view of Megan. As she pushed the door to enter the room a petite curly haired intern passed by. "Of course, I'll get the physician right away," she said as she excused herself.

"Hi," Ashley muttered.

Julie and Nancy turned towards her. The room was single occupancy. That wasn't a good sign, Ashley thought. Since meeting Megan's grandfather, it was apparent to Ashley that Julie looked more like her father, but at that moment, seeing them both with tear-stained faces, puffy eyes and the same distressed look, they resembled each other more than ever.

Nancy was the first to embrace her. As soon as she felt Nancy's arms wrap around her body Ashley began to sob. Julie joined them; all three sobbed uncontrollably. She found some comfort, however small, in knowing that they felt the same way. They understood her pain. She didn't have to pretend to be strong with them.

"I'm sorry." She swiped at her face.

"You have to let it out, sweetheart," Nancy said.

They eventually let go, stepping aside to reveal the reason she was there, her beautiful Megan. Her reason. Her person. Lying there she was almost unrecognisable from the girl Ashley had known. She was covered with tubes and machines, each one playing its part in keeping her alive. The beautiful green eyes that once widened with amazement at the Rockefeller Christmas Tree were now black with bruises. Megan's athletic arms that could propel a basketball effortlessly through the air, lay limp, lifeless and covered in tubes. The flawless lips she'd kissed a week earlier were now pressed against the outside of the tube placed carefully down her throat.

Unlike the old woman two floors down who'd lived a long life, Megan was too young to forfeit hers. She had the potential for a full, happy, healthy, successful life ahead of her, but life was cruel.

"Meg . . . Oh God . . . baby what happened to you?" Ashley sat down beside her, cradling her hand against her face. She looked back tearfully at Julie for some explanation. "What happened?"

"A man walking by witnessed it happen. He called the ambulance. Apparently, she was crossing the road. There was no traffic control sign, but the driver didn't stop. The witness said the man behind the wheel was driving recklessly. He hit her . . . and he . . ." Julie sobbed, ". . . he just drove away."

"Did they catch him?" Ashley snapped, the anger pulsating through her veins.

"The man who witnessed it gave a statement and took the license plate number; they're still looking for the driver. I'm not sure if they have him yet."

"I hope the bastard burns in hell," Nancy declared.

"I'll kill him . . . if she doesn't . . ." Ashley dropped her head to rest on the edge of the bed. The tears were uncontrollable now. ". . . if she doesn't make it . . . I'll kill him."

The beep of the monitor and the compression noise of oxygen making its way through the tube into Megan's mouth sounded so loud. Despite the background noise of a busy hospital, everything was so much louder than it seemed on TV. It was all Ashley could focus on, every beep, and every hum emitting from the machine reminded her of where she was, what was at stake and the overall severity of the situation.

A middle-aged Indian woman with shoulder length black hair neatly tucked behind her ears entered; her smile was soft.

"Hello, I'm Dr. Alberty and I'll be in charge of Megan's care," she said in a strong Boston accent.

They all turned their attention towards her. There was real sympathy behind her eyes as she spoke. She made a conscious effort to make eye contact with everyone in the room as she adjusted the stethoscope around her neck and reached for the chart at the end of the bed.

"Can you tell me what's going on, please," Julie asked.

"May I ask who the next of kin is?"

"I'm her aunt. Her parents live in England, so I'm responsible for her here."

"Okay." Dr. Alberty examined the chart, made a quick observation and placed the chart back at the foot of the bed. She gestured for Julie and Nancy to take a seat.

"When she came in last night, we had to perform emergency surgery which allowed us to stop the internal bleeding. She suffered a couple of broken ribs. Her right ankle was severely damaged by the impact; we assume it was the right side of her body that took the initial blow because her right arm has significant damage. Luckily there was no severe break." Ashley looked at the cast supporting Megan's leg and the strap holding her arm in position. She shot the ball with her right arm, Ashley thought.

"She stabilised after that. We put her in an induced coma due to the swelling around her brain, but we weren't overly concerned about that. Swelling of the brain is quite common in such traumatic circumstances. From the scans, it looks to be a mix of fluid and inflammatory cells. We expect that to reduce over the next 2–3 days."

"Wait, will she have some form of brain damage from that?" Julie asked.

"We don't suspect any long-term damage to her brain. It is something we need to monitor closely, but in these circumstances nine out of ten patients recover fully. We don't suspect permanent memory loss or her ability to function or think normally to be permanently affected."

There was a sigh of relief from all three of them.

"However." Ashley's heart dropped. "In the early hours of this morning we had to rush her back into surgery. We discovered severe renal trauma."

"Sorry, what is renal trauma?" Nancy asked.

"This is what we call injury to the kidney caused by an outside force. Your kidneys are guarded by your back muscle and your rib cage. Upon impact with the vehicle, the ribs on her right side punctured her liver. This ruptured her organ and caused severe blood loss. We had to perform another emergency surgery to try and preserve the kidney on her right side. Unfortunately, it was too badly damaged which meant the only option was to remove it."

Ashley tried to process the information; she replaced the big words with more understandable language which helped, but she didn't understand. She wanted to scream—*Just tell me she's going to be okay*—That's all they were waiting for. Some confirmation that she would be *okay*.

"Can she survive with one kidney?" Julie held on to Nancy's arm. Each second their faces drained of optimism.

"Yes, healthy adults can live a normal life with just one kidney, but that one kidney needs to be healthy in order to perform the work of two kidneys," Dr. Alberty clarified. She looked sympathetically towards Megan who lay completely unaware.

"But her second kidney isn't healthy, is it?" Ashley asked. That bit she understood, the doctor's face said everything she needed to know.

"No. The second kidney is failing as a result of the internal trauma. Her blood isn't filtering the way it should. We had to place a catheter in her left leg for quick access to her bloodstream. That way we could immediately start performing hemodialysis. The machine to your right is filtering out her blood and returning clean blood back into her system." She pointed towards a grey machine with red tubes. "The tubes are extracting her blood as we speak."

"What are the long-term effects? Will her kidney recover?" Nancy asked.

"A kidney once severely damaged won't recover. Dialysis can do the job of a healthy kidney, but it requires three visits a week to the hospital and in the best case will give 10–15 years until a kidney transplant becomes the only remaining option."

"That's not an option. She's a professional basketball player. It's her life; it's all she's ever known. Surely there has to be something else you can do?" Julie challenged.

Dr. Alberty nodded. "I understand. This comes as a shock. There is the option of a transplant. Normally if a patient is O positive which is the most common blood type, then we have a high chance of matching them with a doner on our list. However, Megan's blood type is B positive which means the odds drop significantly as only 8% of the population have that blood type."

Nancy sobbed. "How long is the waiting list?"

"Patients wait 2–3 years on average, but it can be fewer."

"What about family members? Can we be tested? I'll donate my kidney," Julie said.

"So will I," Ashley added without hesitation.

"And me," Nancy added.

Dr. Alberty smiled softly, but behind the smile Ashley sensed the diminishing hope.

"We can test all of you right away if that's what you'd like to do."

"What are the chances of one of us being a match? Her parents are flying in today. They'll test too. One of us must be a match," Julie said.

"There is no guarantee with these things. I don't want to promise anything that I can't guarantee, but we can test and go from there."

"And basketball?" Ashley asked.

"Transplants take a considerable amount of recovery time. Every patient is different, but I'm afraid Megan won't be playing basketball for a long time."

Dr. Alberty waited patiently as they digested the information.

"I'm sorry that I can't give you better news right now. Do you have any more questions before I leave?"

"When can we get tested?" Julie asked.

"I will inform the phlebotomist that we want three blood samples as soon as possible. If we get a match there are other tests we will need to carry out, but we can discuss those after we get the results. Anything else?"

"I don't think so. Thank you, Doctor, for explaining everything," Nancy said.

"Once again, I am truly sorry I don't have good news for you right now. The intern that was here earlier will take care of anything you need. I will check back later to see how she's progressing." Dr. Alberty gripped Nancy's shoulder as she left.

Ashley softly stroked Megan's forehead, carefully avoiding a bandage that covered one of the many lacerations she'd endured.

I know you're in there somewhere, Ashley thought. Her body was broken, bruised and her chances of a full recovery would decrease with every passing hour, but she was in there. She was fighting for her second chance. There had to be a way to save her.

"This can't be how our relationship ends," Ashley whispered. "It's not fair. It can't be."

9

Ashley

The vending machine was typically a last resort for finding food. A selection of chips and sugary beverages did the trick when sugar levels were low, but they didn't fulfil the body. Strange really, hospitals not having nutritional snacks; then again, the person buying the snacks was never the sick one, Ashley thought. She purchased a bag of Cheetos and a can of Pepsi. After the blood tests she needed something to stop her feeling like she was about to pass out.

The combination of needles, blood and the overall shock of what she'd heard the day before made her feel extremely light-headed.

She slumped on the uncomfortable metal bench beside the machine; she was only at the end of the corridor if anything was to happen. Megan's parents had arrived late the previous night. Neither had left her side since. Nancy and Julie had reluctantly gone home to freshen up and make a few phone calls. They needed to update Megan's coach, agent and extended family members of her condition. As guilty as they felt for leaving, there was no use in five people being constantly sat at her bedside.

Ashley had taken the next few days off work. She'd explained to Sonia that it was a family emergency and she'd obliged her request. Ashley was in no frame of mind to write a rom-com style article full of passion, true love and the best cliches in the world when the girl she loved was lying unconscious in a hospital bed.

She cracked the can of Pepsi. The cold fizzy liquid quenched her thirst and left her feeling refreshed. When she opened the pack of Cheetos, the crunchy corn puff snack emitted a strong smell which left her feeling nauseous.

The electronic double doors to her left propelled open. Sofia stormed in. When their eyes met, Ashley immediately noticed the look of concern on her face turn to a scowl. She stood to greet her. Ashley was concerned she'd only just been informed of Megan's condition, and she would no doubt have the same barrage of questions Ashley had.

"You've got some nerve," Sofia snapped through clenched teeth.

Ashley planted her feet firmly as Sofia barged past her. She made the extra effort to knock Ashley off balance. "What the hell Sofia?" Ashley's arm flew backwards with the momentum of Sofia's shoulder hitting her. Ashley grabbed a hold of her arm as she tried to walk away. "What's wrong with you?"

"This is all your fault," Sofia scolded. Ripping her arm from Ashley's grasp.

"I don't understand . . ." She began, but Sofia interrupted.

"Do you know where she got hit?"

"She was in Midtown, near Chelsea."

"Why the hell was Megan in Midtown on a Saturday night?" The question hadn't really crossed her mind. She assumed she'd gone for a run, or maybe a walk to clear her head. The relevance of her location didn't matter at the time. Megan's recovery had been the only topic of importance.

"The only reason she was there was because of you. She came to surprise you!" The rage behind Sofia's words caused Ashley to flinch.

"Wait . . . what?" She mumbled. "How do you know that?"

"She called me after she'd seen you with Madison."

Ashley stared motionless straight ahead. Her eyebrows curled towards each other. Confused. "With Madison?"

"Can't you just stick to one woman? Why is that so hard for you? Do you enjoy playing them off each other?" Sofia growled.

"It's not like that . . ." Ashley recalled Saturday night and her avoidance of Madison right up until the moment they had their overdue conversation. *Had Megan witnessed that?*

"I bought her a drink. We had a chat about us hopefully being friends again one day. I told her about me and Megan. There was nothing more to it."

Sofia's face remained unchanged. "Megan saw her kiss you." She pointed out.

"On the cheek! She kissed me on the cheek. It was a goodbye gesture . . ."

Sofia interrupted yet again, "Of course you're going to say that."

"She'd told me a minute before she kissed me on the cheek that she wanted me to be happy and that there were no hard feelings." She shook her head. "I swear to you. Whatever Megan thought she saw, she was wrong. I would never . . ."

"Do that to her? Because that's not something you do? Give me a break Ashley."

Sofia rolled her eyes.

"You're being unfair."

"Am I?"

"Yes."

"You do realise that she wouldn't be in this position right now if it wasn't for you."

"Yes! Okay! I fucking know!" Ashley yelled before lowering her tone as two nurses walked by. "I know this is my fault." She slumped onto the metal bench. The woman she loved was hooked up to machines, each one working hard to keep her body functioning, and up until ten minutes ago the man driving the car had been solely to blame. The police would catch up with him. He'd serve his time in prison; the duration would more than likely be determined by the outcome of Megan's condition. Ashley hoped for a shorter sentence, not because that's what he deserved, but because that would mean that Megan survived.

What she hadn't anticipated was her own involvement. She'd played the doting girlfriend for the past two days without knowing that she was just as much to blame as the man who hit her. *What would Megan's parents think? Nancy? Julie? Would they blame her too?*

Sofia shook her hand in Ashley's direction. "I swear to God, Ashley. If she doesn't recover from this, I'll never forgive you. I don't care if you're telling the truth or not."

She stormed down the corridor and straight past Megan's room. Ashley could have corrected her, but she figured an extra few steps to cool off wouldn't harm anyone.

Every part of Ashley's body shook so hard she thought it might crumble and diminish into nothing more than a pile of dust, soon to be swept away by the janitor.

If only Megan had told her she was coming. If only she'd had the warning to distance herself from Madison. She could've been awaiting her arrival outside Midtown 101. They could've celebrated Jason's birthday, gone home together with a pizza and spent the early hours of Sunday morning in each other's arms. The fact that she slept comfortably whilst Megan lay in the hospital having her organs removed and her bones set, whilst her body bled out, left Ashley reeling with guilt. Suddenly, she felt sick; she ran for the bin, hurling up liquid. Sofia's words echoed in her ears.

It's all your fault.

***

The smell of hospital disinfectant filled Ashley's lungs. The room full of people who loved Megan was silent. Nancy and Julie had returned. Sofia left soon after their bust-up. It became apparent that meaningless chitchat was just that, meaningless. What did it matter how work was going, what you had for lunch or what you were planning on doing for Thanksgiving. Ashley realised how irrelevant it all was when something horrific happened. When someone you loved was fighting for their life, words failed you.

She stared at the monitor. The beeping sound didn't waver. It soon became part of the background noise. A tap on her watch indicated the time. As the silence was coming close to thirty minutes, in walked Dr. Alberty.

Everyone stood and turned towards her like the president of the United States had just entered the room, or Oprah.

"I have some news. We have a match for Megan." Dr. Alberty scouted the room, her gaze finally falling on Nancy.

"Nancy, you're a match,"

Michael's face turned to one of concern. "Where any others a match? Or just my mom?"

"It was just Nancy. It would have been ideal to have more than one option, as I said earlier, but to have one option at all with Megan's blood type is good."

"Either way it's great news," Nancy said. "So, what happens now?" She asked. Eager to speed along the process. Ashley admired her courage.

"Next, we have to take you for tissue typing. The better HLA match you are with Megan, the more chance of the transplant being successful over a long period of time. It's important we test for the presence of HLA antibodies before any transplant is carried out. If the levels are too high in either you or Megan, the kidney may not be compatible. After that we'll need to do what's called a serum crossmatch. We will mix cells from you with Megan's serum. If Megan's serum has antibodies against your cells at high levels the cells will be destroyed. This is what we call a positive crossmatch, and it would mean the transplant would not be able to take place."

"What are the chances of that happening?" Michael asked, as he grasped Nancy's hand tightly.

"There is a 10–15% chance of the kidney not being compatible, but every patient is different. We don't know how Megan's body will react, so we will always take an informed approach."

Dr. Alberty paused for any questions. The room remained silent. She continued, "Nancy, I need to talk with you about the procedure and the potential risks that come with your age and your current medical condition. This is something we need to discuss in depth before we can continue."

Nancy nodded. *Her current medical condition?* Ashley heard that loud and clear. Something was wrong.

"I have two other patients that need my urgent attention, but I will send for you once I am available. Is that okay?"

"Yes, of course. Thank you," Nancy said.

"Do you have any questions before I leave?"

Megan's mom had been silent throughout the exchange. She'd barely said two words since her arrival the night before. She was the picture of a broken woman.

"Doctor . . . why hasn't my daughter woken up yet?" They all looked at Megan. She lay in the exact same position she'd been in when they arrived. There were no signs of movement, not a twitch of the mouth, or a wiggle of the finger to let them know she was still in there, still fighting. The only movement came from the machine; shoots of green showed her vital signs rising and falling consistently. The readout showed a pattern that meant she was strong. She was going to be okay, at least that's what Ashley hoped.

"Mrs Davis, your daughter suffered a traumatic injury. Her brain swelled considerably, causing the fluid to push up against her skull. After reviewing the scans my prognosis is still the same as yesterday. I don't believe there is any bleeding on the brain, which is a good thing. However, to protect the brain we have to keep your daughter in a medically induced coma. This is the best chance we have of making sure she makes a full recovery. The swelling has reduced ever so slightly, but her internal organs have become infected. Infection of the central nervous system in her current situation would likely cause your daughter to fall into a natural coma as well as a list of other complications. The best thing we can do now is keep her in the condition she's currently in and continue to monitor her closely."

Amanda sobbed. "My baby girl." She held her daughter's hand delicately, trying not to dislodge the cable attached to her finger.

"Is she going to be okay? Please tell me she's going to be okay. She's my only child. She's my little girl. I can't lose her." Michael walked to the other side of the bed to hold his wife.

Ashley felt a lump in her throat; the idea of losing Megan wasn't something she could comprehend, but what must it be like for her parents? They'd watched their beautiful baby girl grow into the successful, kind, thoughtful young woman that she was. They'd guided her through life as best they could and tried to keep her from harm's way. Their one collective goal in life was to make sure she was okay. And now, they watched in agony as the realisation of her condition hit. This wasn't something they could save her from. It wasn't something they could take away or make better by putting a Band-Aid over her bruised knee like they did when she was a child. They had to watch helplessly and pray for a miracle.

They say that even a non-religious person prays when they're faced with the unthinkable. They pray for a miracle even though they've never believed in miracles. They pray for an almighty being to take away the sorrow, or to rip a loved one back from the jaws of death. What else can you do when it seems completely hopeless?

"I assure you she is in the very best hands, and we will do everything within our power to make sure she has every chance at making a full recovery," Dr. Alberty said. She had experience talking with patients. Ashley could tell she'd had many difficult conversations. The way she held herself, knowing when to show empathy and sympathy, and she never appeared rushed when speaking. She was concise and knowledgeable, making sure the family understood the situation. She aired on the side of caution, knowing to focus on the positives and the negatives. She didn't give the family false hope, but gave them the information so their expectations were realistic. Dr. Alberty couldn't promise a full recovery. She couldn't promise them that Megan would be okay because there were never any guarantees.

When Dr. Alberty left, Ashley turned towards Nancy. "What did the doctor mean when she said your current medical condition?"

Nancy reached her arm around Ashley's waist. For the first time since they'd met she thought Nancy looked old. Despite being almost eighty, Nancy had aged like a Hollywood actress with access to monthly Botox. Ashley often wished she could bottle up Nancy's DNA and use it as face cream. Now, the stress of the situation caused her fresh complexion to look drawn. Her wide youthful eyes looked sunken and tired. Her wrinkles, natural for a woman of her age, had become even more prominent.

"Don't you worry about me, sweetheart. I'll be fine." Nancy squeezed Ashley's hip and wandered over to Megan's bedside once again.

What did that mean? What was she not telling her? It wasn't her place to force the conversation. After all, Nancy was Megan's grandmother not hers.

Before the hospital, the last time she'd seen Nancy was at the wedding. A lot can change in five weeks, but her change in appearance left Ashley wondering if it was simply worry or something more.

10

Nancy

In 1950s New York.

Growing up in Queens, Nancy had access to everything she could want. The large department stores, Broadway shows, movie theatres and even the local beaches. It was never a case of—*What do we do now?*—that was what she struggled to understand about the youth of today.

She remembered exiting World War II with no damage to the city. She remembered streets with so few cars that she and the local children could use them as playgrounds. Candy stores began to emerge every few blocks. When she turned thirteen, she began to look after her younger sister whilst her mom worked in the factory and her dad went to work in an office downtown. Provided she cared for her sibling with little to no concern, her father would treat her to some Chuckles jelly candy and liquorice chews every Saturday.

Every Friday, as a family, they would go to the local Horn & Hardart restaurant. The restaurant chain was a common sight around the city. She would toss a few nickels in the slot below a glass window and have access to a prepared meal. It was fast food in the 1950s. Nancy remembered the day the final H&H automat closed its doors in 1991. The stiff competition from the likes of McDonald's became too much for the ninety-year-old company. She'd travelled back from North Carolina in 1991 to sample the food one final time.

The countless hours spent jumping rope with her friends, and the long summer hours on stoops dancing to the latest hits to blast from her father's record player, were the days she cherished now more than ever. Like it was yesterday, she remembered her ears glued to the radio, taking in black voices loaded with intense emotion. The likes of Nat King Cole, Chuck Berry and Fats Domino left her feeling euphoric.

Sundays were important in Nancy's household. Her parents were devout Catholics. They went to the Sunday service at Our Lady of Lourdes Roman Catholic Church every week. Nancy's father was good friends with the pastor. He came to their house for dinner every Thursday night with his wife and two children. She loved those dinners because their eldest boy, Jim, was her age. He turned out to be the first boy she ever kissed. Every Sunday after church they'd run to the local bakery for fresh cream-filled donuts. Life was grand.

Susan, Nancy's mother, tried desperately to set her up with Jim. As they reached the age of seventeen, the comments became a daily occurrence, "What about Jim? do you like him?" or "What's wrong with Jim? He's the pastor's son." At the time, Nancy just wasn't interested.

The summer after that, Nancy met Christopher. Jim became a distant memory, and that infuriated her parents. She'd never gone steady with anyone, not properly, not until Christopher. He changed everything for her. Luckily, he sat beside her now, clutching her hand in his own as they waited patiently for Dr. Alberty to arrive.

The fond memories of her childhood changed once she left New York. Her grandfather had come from North Carolina to collect her in his black 1955 Bentley S1. The return trip to Charlotte took the better part of a day. She loved her grandparents, or what she knew of them. They had a lot of money, but her mother didn't talk about them often. When Nancy's mother lost her job, the family could barely afford to put food on the table, but her parents never once asked her grandparents for help. They would visit during the holidays, but her parents never really seemed pleased to see them.

Nancy found out later that Susan had left the household when she was twenty years of age because her father used to beat her mother and she'd feared she might be next. Luckily, despite her mother's ludicrous decision to send her to live with her abusive grandfather and her religiously obsessive grandmother, Nancy managed to survive the two years of arbitrary under their roof before she met Robert Davis.

Robert was a kind man. They'd met at the local hospital where Nancy volunteered. Robert was a training physician. The more she got to know him, the more she volunteered. Slowly but surely the idea of a reunion with Christopher slipped to the back of her mind. She built a life with Robert. He promised her the world, and two children quickly followed. In the seventies they purchased a dream home for their family. Nancy was happy, for the most part. She didn't have to work; Robert earned enough to allow her to raise their children without financial worries. Her grandparents died in the early seventies, one year apart. Her mother died in 1986 followed by her father in 1990. They both died relatively young. Susan died from a brain tumour and Thomas from a heart attack. Living through her mother's experience had prepared Nancy for the news she'd received earlier that year. As soon as the Doctor sat her down and said, "There's a tumour." She knew she wouldn't survive it.

Just before their vow renewal she'd begun vomiting frequently. The headaches she'd experienced on and off for a while grew more acute and persistent. That's when she knew her body was trying to tell her that something wasn't right. She went to the doctor with Julie. A week later, after multiple tests and scans, her condition was confirmed. It was a malignant gliomas brain tumour. The probability of surviving longer than five years fell to 36% with an average life expectancy closer to 12–18 months.

The doctor's office was well lit, open, and spacious with two large grey chairs at one side of the desk. The back wall had an abundance of natural light with a run of large windows allowing the space to feel welcoming. It wasn't your typical consult room; it wasn't bland and sterile. There were no curtains separating the examination table from the rest of room and no large sets of drawers containing swabs, plastic gloves, or specimen bags. All those things felt redundant in this room, like it was specifically designed for delivering bad news.

They'd been sat waiting for five minutes before Dr. Alberty entered the room.

"I apologise for keeping you waiting, Nancy. I had an emergency surgery that overran." She never seemed to rush. There was a calming aura about her, and Nancy liked her. She flicked on her computer and pulled a file from the cabinet.

"It's Christopher, isn't it? I don't believe we've met. You're Nancy's husband?"

"I am. It's nice to meet you Doctor." He extended his hand across the desk.

"Please, call me Helen." Her gaze turned towards Nancy. "Nancy, how are you feeling?"

"I feel like an old woman, but I am an old woman, so that's nothing new," She smiled softly.

"I disagree." Dr. Alberty looked amused. She opened the file and began scanning its contents. "I had your consultant over at Presbyterian send me your file. I can see here that you refused Chemotherapy. Is that still your decision?"

"Yes."

"Can I ask why?"

"My cancer can't be cured, Doctor. I have already come to terms with the fact that I'm dying. Chemotherapy can only help slow the spread. My quality of life in the remaining time I have is more important to me."

She looked to Christopher; he looked sad, her instinct was to comfort him. She'd found strength in having a terminal disease. As soon as the doctors had diagnosed her, she'd known what the outcome would be, but she hadn't wept. She didn't want pity. She refused to let people feel sorrow for her, until it was time to go. That was her reasoning for not telling the people she knew and loved. Only Julie, Michael and Christopher were aware of her condition. She battled with that decision for several months. She felt selfish at times for refusing treatment, and for refusing to allow her family the proper time to accept and come to terms with such a life-altering situation.

"I understand." Dr. Alberty continued to study the file.

"Will that affect my being eligible to donate a kidney?" She'd already done her research. Well, she'd asked Julie to. Nancy was not a technology expert. When she'd asked why her laptop had an apple on it, her granddaughter, Megan, had almost fallen from her chair in a fit of laughter.

"We would not normally accept organs from anyone with an actively spreading cancer. However, your tumour is a primary brain tumour, which means it originated from the tissues of the brain, and it hasn't spread beyond the brain stem. This means it hasn't infected any of your other organs."

"Does that qualify as an exception?"

"After reviewing the literature for organ donors with Megan's blood type and taking into consideration the current organ shortage, we feel the risk of transmission to the recipient appears to be very low. This allows us to consider you as a potential donor in this case. There are only a few considerations. I must be able to confidently say that by donating the organ you're not putting your own health at unnecessary risk and that you're donating a healthy organ that is unlikely to reject or transmit infection from your body to the recipients."

"So, you'd be willing to do it?"

"We need to do the necessary tests, but provided your kidney is healthy, yes, we have a case to follow through with the transplant."

"That's great." She nodded, feeling optimistic.

"However . . ." Dr. Alberty crossed her hands on the desk. "I am not a neurosurgeon. I can only base my decision on what I see in front of me. Naturally, your chances of complication during a procedure like what we are proposing increase as you get older. As you reach eighty years of age there is also a higher risk of respiratory complications whilst under anaesthesia."

"In your honest opinion, am I too old?" Nancy asked.

"There is no age limit for organ donation. I have operated on young children, and I have operated on older adults, eighty-three being the eldest."

"Did they survive?"

"She did, yes. Not without complications, but the transplant was successful. However, the recovery time doubles, if not triples, from that of a young healthy adult."

Christopher cleared his throat. "What are the odds of a serious complication?"

"What he means is . . . what are the chances of me dying?" Nancy said matter-of-factly.

"I don't like it when you say that," Christopher said.

"I know, but it's going to happen one day, darling."

Dr. Alberty hesitated to answer the question.

"In my experience, I would say there is a 20% chance of complications. If you were forty years of age, it would be 5%. The risk is certainly higher, and that is something you can take time to consider before you go ahead."

"There is nothing to consider."

Christopher placed his hand on Nancy's arm. "My love, surely, we should talk about this?"

"My granddaughter's life is at risk, as far as I am concerned, there is nothing to discuss."

Christopher didn't argue. She'd made up her mind. "How do we proceed?"

Dr. Alberty spoke at length about the benefits and the risks of the operation, what was involved, what anaesthetic would be used and how it would look from start to finish. Then she reached for a piece of paper from Nancy's file.

"This is the consent form for the operation. I need this written record signed to say you agree to the planned operation and you're fully aware of everything I have discussed with you today." She handed Nancy a pen. She signed without wavering.

"We have the tissue typing and the serum crossmatch to do next. I can get you in first thing in the morning and hopefully have the results back the following day."

"If all that comes back as it should, when will the operation take place?"

"I can have the theatre ready as soon as Saturday. Megan's condition is critical; we have to monitor her and determine whether she's strong enough to survive the operation. That will be a deciding factor."

"Okay doctor, thank you." Nancy stood to leave, she felt light-headed, but she didn't complain. Her limbs felt weak, but that was normal as of late. She'd put it down to old age, but she knew the brain tumour was slowly but surely rearing its ugly head.

The doctor could've told her the survival rate was 50/50 or 30/70 against her, but her concern for her own health came nowhere near the concern for her granddaughter's health. A little fatigue and brain fog wouldn't force her to rethink, but it might force the doctors to reconsider, and that was her concern. She was glad Christopher had asked about complications. It would give him some clarity or, at least, some hope. Nancy knew that whilst Christopher would pray for hers and Megan's recovery, that night, she would only pray for one thing—her granddaughter to live a long and happy life, whatever the cost.

In a private conversation with Dr. Alberty an hour before Christopher arrived at the hospital, Nancy had already put in motion the DNR (do-not-resuscitate) order.

Now all she could do was wait.

11

Ashley

Ashley appeared at the foot of Megan's hospital bed, but Megan wasn't there. The sheets had been removed. Smears of blood on the mattress underneath spelt out the words *I love you.* The floor was covered in gauze, surgical equipment and bloodstained scrubs. The ECG machine lay on its side with one constant line; the persistent beep pierced her ears. The noise grew louder. She placed her fingers in her ears and ran from room to room searching. *She must still be in the hospital.* Ashley ran down empty corridors filled with bloody footprints; each one guiding her towards the exit.

Ashley's adrenaline saw her sprinting through New York City. She had no destination in mind. The beep followed, taunting her. She stormed into Nancy's bar screaming "Where's Megan?" at the top of her lungs. Nobody turned around. Nobody acknowledged her presence.

The woman behind the bar looked familiar, but she wasn't sure where she'd seen her. When she got up close, she recognised the woman; it was Sofia. Her shoulder-length dark hair had new blue highlights. The lines underneath her eyes were deep and gloomy. A mixture of piercings covered her face, and a large prominent scar curved from above her left eye all the way down to her jawline.

"Sofia?"

"You did this," She yelled. "You did this."

Ashley fell backwards. Bottles of alcohol began to smash one by one along the back wall of the bar. The glass shattered around Sofia's face, but she didn't flinch.

"You killed my best friend," she screamed.

The vibration shook the room, but still none of the customers paid her any attention. Sofia turned the volume up on the music system as "Died in Your Arms Tonight" by Cutting Crew erupted through the speakers. It sent Ashley backpedalling through the door and onto the streets of Manhattan again.

The music disappeared as soon as the door slammed shut behind her. Immediately, the unrelenting beep of the hospital machine returned. "Megan," she yelled, "Megan, where are you?" The streets were deserted, cars abandoned, litter strewn across the sidewalk and then the footprints reappeared. In amongst the candy wrappers and fast-food bags she spotted the bloody footprints she'd seen at the hospital. They led her directly to a large black wooden door, she slammed the knocker against the wood, knocking, one, two, three times.

A man appeared in a tuxedo; his hair was buzzed like a military man's. When his face emerged fully from the shadow of the door, she noticed his features. It was Michael, but he looked thirty years older. His face was drawn, his beard was scruffy and untamed.

"You're not allowed in here. Not after what you did," he said.

"Michael, what happened to Megan? Please, I need to know."

"You killed my daughter. Leave." The door slammed in her face. She fell backwards, stumbling on the curb's edge.

Suddenly, her vision momentarily turned black, and she found herself on the floor of Julie's apartment. A barefooted figure dressed in a basketball jersey wandered down the hall. Ashley watched the long brown hair sway from left to right; the back of her jersey spelt out the surname *Davis*. Ashley crawled to her feet, but her feet felt like concrete blocks; they wouldn't move.

"Megan. Wait for me. Megan, I'm sorry." Ashley's throat tightened. The words sounded strained. No matter how hard she tried to yell, the words came out barely audible. She scratched and clawed her way to the door at the end of the hall, searching for Megan.

She pushed the door open, and she was back in the hospital. The bloodbath had been cleaned up, and a new patient lay in Megan's bed.

"Where the hell is Megan? Will someone tell me what the fuck is going on?"

Dr. Alberty stopped talking to the new patient's family members and turned sharply towards the door.

"She's dead!"

She's dead. She's dead. She's dead.

Ashley awoke suddenly, frantically she scanned the room. *Where am I?* When her eyes adjusted to the light, she didn't immediately recognise the burnt-orange bed covers. *This isn't my bed.*

She shot upright. Her t-shirt stuck to her body, and she felt perspiration clammy against her hand as she reached for her neck, adjusting it left and then right. She felt stiff.

Am I still dreaming? Out of nowhere a hand touched her arm causing her to jolt and lash out. "Fuck!"

"Woah, it's me. It's Emily."

Ashley's hand flew to her chest, the beat of her heart was thudding through her bones. "Jesus, Em."

"Sorry." Emily chuckled.

"Why am I in your bed?"

"You couldn't sleep, so you crawled into my bed at 2:00 a.m. and decided to help me not sleep as well." Emily reached for the bedside lamp.

"I just had the weirdest dream," Ashley said.

"You've been having them all night."

"I have?"

"Yep, almost every hour. It's been super fun sleeping next to you," she jested. Emily plumped her pillow against the headboard and sat upright, her eyes squinting so much that only the tiniest bit of her inner eye could be seen poking through.

"I'm sorry," Ashley said.

"Don't be. What kind of best friend would I be if I couldn't take a beating from you in your sleep?" She grabbed Ashley's pillow and placed it against the headboard to match her own, gesturing for her to join.

"I'm sorry for being so sweaty." Ashley grimaced, she removed her t-shirt, slightly embarrassed by the off-white bralette that was five years old and too comfy to throw away.

"I will be washing the bedding today. That is a fact."

Ashley glanced towards the alarm clock on Emily's bedside table. She'd teased her about the old-school alarm for years. Despite technology advancing considerably and most people trusting their mobile phones to wake them up in the morning; Emily didn't take that risk. She often set three alarms: her personal mobile, her work mobile and her small black portable alarm clock—she was thorough. The clock read 8:09 a.m.

"Shouldn't you be at work already?"

Emily yawned. "I told you the other day, my boss is on holiday in the Maldives so I can work from home if I need to."

"You do all his dirty work for him, and he doesn't even let you go with him to the Maldives?"

"I'm not sure his wife would approve."

"Oh, so he's taking the wife and not the mistress this time?"

"Exactly, he has to share out the holidays. Besides, as much as I'd love a trip to the Maldives, it is nice when he's not here. I still have to coordinate his life, but not to the same extent. And it means I can be here with you, in this lovely sweaty bed getting kicked repeatedly whilst I sleep."

"Win win," Ashley said. She smiled, observing her reflection in the mirror on the wall to her left. She looked like someone trying to be positive on the surface, but she knew that deep down she was completely broken and lost.

"Do you want to tell me about your dream?" Emily asked.

"It was more of a nightmare really."

"Was I in it?"

"No, you're in most of my nightmares, but not this one."

Emily hit her playfully. "That's not nice." She reached for her unruly blonde locks and pulled them back with the hair tie around her wrist. "Did it involve Megan?"

Ashley nodded.

"Bad?"

Ashley nodded again.

"Don't want to talk about it?"

She shook her head. "Not really."

"Okay." Emily could be like a dog with a bone when prompted, but she also knew when to leave things alone. "Are you going to see Megan this morning?"

"Of course."

"Tomorrow's the operation, right?" Emily asked.

"Yeah, Nancy's results came back yesterday. She's a good match."

"That's great, right?"

"Yeah, it's really good." Ashley said.

"You don't sound like it's good."

Ashley let out a long breath. "I just worry, for Megan, and for Nancy. What if something goes wrong?"

"Have the doctors said that's a possibility?" Emily asked.

"There's always a possibility, isn't there? They have to give you the best and worst-case scenarios. It's just Nancy's age and the fact that Megan hasn't even woken up yet. It's scary." She turned to face her best friend with tears in her eyes. "I'm scared, Em."

"I know. Come here." Emily pulled Ashley into her lap, gently stroking her tangled mess of hair and carefully unravelling any knots with her fingers.

"She'll be okay, right?" Ashley tilted her head back to look at Emily. She needed a crystal ball; but failing that she needed comfort, just a ray of light at the end of the dark tunnel that had consumed her for almost a week.

"I wish I knew," she admitted. "Do you want to know what I believe?"

Ashley nodded.

"I believe your story isn't over. The world can be cruel, but I don't believe it can be that cruel. The two of you were meant to find each other. I don't care what anyone else says. It has to work out. I don't think I could ever believe in love again if it doesn't."

At first, Ashley couldn't form a response; she let the comments linger, trying to find some solace in Emily's words. "Is someone trying to punish me?"

"Of course not."

"Then why? If there is a god out there, why does he insist on fucking me over this way? I work hard. I pay my taxes. I'm kind, and I don't harass people. I'm not a murderer, and I try to live a good life. I do what's right by my family and my friends. I don't steal. I didn't even cheat on my 11th grade maths test when everyone else had the answers. It's not fair." She sat up again, more agitated with each second that passed.

Emily reached for Ashley's chin with her fingertips, guiding her face so she could look her directly in the eyes.

"Life isn't fair, Ash. All you have to do is turn on the news for five minutes to see how unfair life is. It takes great strength to overcome the things in life that make you want to break down and give up. You have to stay strong . . . for Megan."

"I can't lose her, Em. And the worst thing is, if I do, it's all my fault." She buried her head in her hands.

"Hey!" Emily yelled. "Don't say that. It's not your fault."

"No, Sofia's right."

"Sofia's an idiot."

"Sofia's your girlfriend," Ashley pointed out.

"That's beside the point. Doesn't mean she can't be an idiot. She never should have said those things to you."

"She's just upset."

"So are you. The person to blame for all this is the man driving the car. Why she was there is irrelevant. If you asked me to go to the store right now to get you a bar of chocolate and I got in an accident that wouldn't be your fault. Sometimes we're in the wrong place at the wrong time. It's unfortunate, but it's not your fault."

Ashley considered Emily's point of view. There was no use in blaming herself, but until Megan opened her eyes she undoubtedly would.

The visiting hours at the hospital started at 10:00 a.m. Ashley wanted Megan to wake up surrounded by all the things she loved, so each day she brought something to her hospital room. Currently, her favourite Kobe Bryant jersey hung over the back of the chair next to her bed. She'd taken some Cronuts the day before; Megan wouldn't be able to eat them, but the smell was divine. There was a picture of both of them with her parents; they'd taken it whilst out for dinner in England. Ashley had framed it and set it on Megan's bedside table along with some sports magazines and a bag of candy from Dylan's Candy Bar.

They were all materialistic things. They wouldn't aid in Megan's medical recovery, but if there was a possibility that she could sense what was going on around her, if she could smell, or hear, or have some supernatural out-of-body experience where she could see the hospital room from an outsider's perspective, if there was even a 1% chance of that happening, she would see how much she was loved. She would sense all her favourite things and her favourite people and know that life was worth living. Life was worth fighting for.

12

Nancy

It was Friday evening. Nancy sat in the home office she'd designed when they first moved in. There had been no real need for it at the time; it was an average sized room that needed a purpose. Over the years it had served as more of a library than an office; it was the place she stored all her favourite books. To her right, a black glass cabinet housed her *Nancy Drew* collection. Those books were some of her most prized possessions. The collection was worth an estimated half a million dollars—if it was sold to the right collector.

She hadn't collected them for their monetary value. She'd had the opportunity to sell them on many occasions. She told keen buyers to contact her children in the future; they would soon inherit the collection. She thought people might think she was crazy if she told them the real reason she didn't want to sell was purely because of the joy she felt in owning them. Every week she'd dust the shelves down, removing each book one by one, taking extra care not to bend the cover or accidentally tear the jacket. The books reminded her of a simpler time, sat on the back steps of their bottom floor two-bedroom apartment with her little sister. The place where her father would read to them the latest releases.

Now, as she examined the mahogany office, with the wood floors and the solid oak desk that had once been her father's. She imagined her mother writing a letter; they'd each received one after her passing. The benefit of knowing you're sick is that you're able to say goodbye in whichever way you choose. Her father didn't have that luxury, not that he was a man of many words. The only time he spoke at length was to read from the pages of literature. She pulled out a letter from the small filing drawer in the centre of the desk.

The envelope had yellowed on the edges. The pages were so badly creased that some words were unreadable, but that was irrelevant. She'd reread the letter's contents hundreds of times over the thirty years since her mother had passed. The word's *Grace is God's kindness* were written in ornamental scroll across the front of the envelope.

Her name, *Nancy*, was of English origin, but her mother chose it due to its meaning—Nancy means *grace*. After her mother miscarried her first child, by the grace of God, Nancy blessed the earth. When she reached adulthood and her mother told her the story of her name, she asked why she didn't just call her Grace. As clear as day, she remembered seeing her throw her head back and laugh, before saying, "well you see, the first girlfriend your father ever courted was called Grace." In the 1930s women were just as jealous of their partner's ex-partners as they are in the twenty-first century.

The pen that her mother used to write sat in a black case at the edge of the desk; it was a 1950s Conway Stewart fountain pen. It was one of the many possessions she'd found inside the desk when her father passed. To some it was just a pen, but to Nancy it was the pen that wrote her mother's final words to her, and it was that same pen that would help her write a series of letters to her granddaughter.

There was no fear when she thought about the operation, only peace. She felt peace in knowing that if she didn't make it through, at least, she'd given her granddaughter the opportunity to live. The operation was likely to be a success; Dr. Alberty had told her as much. The internet told her to be positive, and her family remained optimistic about a full recovery for both herself and Megan.

Nancy didn't have many regrets. She simply didn't believe in them. Regret was like self-pity, all you could do was wallow in it, and then what? It didn't change anything. A regret in its purest form was an enormous misuse of energy. She truly believed that. There was, however, one thing she would regret, leaving the earth without saying goodbye to her only grandchild. That wasn't an option. She gathered some lined paper from the desk drawer, lifted the black pen from its case and began writing.

It was effortless, her hand glided across the page. The words formed into sentences and then paragraphs with no indecision.

My Darling,

If you're reading this, it means I am no longer here. When you wake from your extended sleep you will look around the room and see the faces you love so dearly. You will be happy that you get to walk this planet once more. When the overwhelming sensation of being back in this wonderful place we call Earth subsides, when the hugs and kisses and tears of joy slowly falter, you will ask "Where's Gram?" Only then will you realise the faces of the people you love are tear-stained, and not only with joy because you're well again, but with sorrow for me . . .

13

Ashley

Waiting.

That's all Ashley had done for seven days. Agonisingly wait, hour after hour. Every single day she walked into the hospital room where Megan lay, hoping she'd be sat upright, talking and laughing, and that the world would start to feel normal again. It hadn't happened. Today she sat in a private room with Megan's parents, Julie and Christopher. Waiting once again.

She walked towards the coffee machine, her third trip of the day. At this point she didn't even want coffee, but it was something to do, a mundane task. Press a button and watch the machine make a liquified drink. Pretend there was nothing at stake. There was a Starbucks near the entrance to the hospital; she'd noticed it every day on her way in, and despite her love of vanilla lattes, she refused to leave the waiting room and run the risk of missing Dr. Alberty.

The operation time was estimated between three and four hours. The clock on the wall indicated three hours had passed. She hoped the news would come sooner rather than later. The red hard-backed chairs were starting to correct her posture, and she didn't like that.

The silence felt eerie; it reminded Ashley of her regular appearances in eighth grade detention. Mr. Brum, the science teacher, would give out one hour's

detention every time someone spoke out of turn—
Ashley only learnt that after the fifth time. Now, the
silence was the same, but the stakes were higher, and
nobody was writing the same sentence repeatedly in a
notebook like it was going to change anything.

Megan will wake up and make a full recovery.
Megan will wake up and make a full recovery.

She repeated the words over and over in her mind.
She believed there had to be some benefits to thinking
positively. It might cause a small shift in the universe
somewhere.

The people in the room were drained of personality.
The hospital had zapped it from them as soon as they'd
entered through the double doors three hours earlier.
Ashley observed each of them individually. To keep
herself entertained she'd begun playing a game. She
named it *Observation*. If she could correctly guess what
each person in the room was going to do next, she won.
What did she win? Absolutely nothing, but it passed the
time.

Julie stood at least every twenty minutes, pacing
from left to right. Thankfully she'd swapped her high
heels from the day before for a flat pair of trainers, so
the monotonous click clack had stopped. Michael rolled
his head at least once every thirty minutes, letting out a
sigh along with it that let everyone in the room know he
wasn't cut out for waiting. Amanda closed her eyes for
the first two hours; she wasn't sleeping though, Ashley
could tell by the way she held her posture. She wasn't
slumping, snoring, or showing any signs of being in a
deep sleep. Maybe she was meditating, she thought.

After hour number two she began stretching her legs
on the floor like a middle-aged gymnast. Ashley hadn't
predicted that one. Then there was Christopher; he

tapped his foot to some beat that nobody else seemed to be aware of, and he made no eye contact with anyone. He'd been sat staring at the wedding band on his hand for at least an hour.

As well as playing *Observation* in her mind, there were the painfully designed posters on every noticeboard in the room. Each poster had been devised specifically to have an impact on its intended target audience. After hours of staring at the posters Ashley wasn't sure whether to get a flu shot, see a therapist, get checked for STDs or train to be a nurse.

The corridor on the other side of the wooden doors was quiet. Every so often a group of people would pass, and the room would be flooded with sound before falling deathly silent again.

Ashley heard a set of footsteps shuffling along the sheet vinyl outside. The footsteps sounded different. They slowed as they got closer, and the tortured creak of the waiting room door gave way to Dr. Alberty.

She didn't smile, instead, she took a long deep breath.

Five sets of eyes shared panic-stricken glances with each other before settling on Dr. Alberty's unchanged face. Before she opened her mouth to say the words, Ashley felt as though a ten-ton rock had been slammed repeatedly into her chest.

"Mr. and Mrs. Davis, we believe the transplant has been successful. The nurses are closely monitoring Megan as we speak. She will need around-the-clock care over these next twenty-four hours to make sure her body accepts the organ and that it begins to work on its own without the support of machines."

Amanda grabbed hold of Michael's arm—sudden elation. Ashley felt her whole body relax. A tentative smile crept over her lips. Ashley however, observed Dr. Alberty's body language and knew there was more to come.

"However . . ."

Ashley gulped.

"I also need to inform you that there were some unforeseen complications." The split second of joy now came crumbling down.

"What do you mean?" Michael asked.

"The initial extraction from Nancy to Megan went as planned, but with any surgery there is extra pressure on the body to continue functioning at a high level. When we closed the incision in Nancy's abdomen, her vitals dropped; her blood pressure decreased and her heartbeat became irregular; we tried to counteract these things using medication, but she went into cardiac arrest."

It took a few seconds for her ears to comprehend the words. "I don't understand," Julie said. "Is my mom okay?"

"Nancy's heart stopped beating. As soon as that happened there was nothing we could do. The signed DNR stopped us from performing cardiopulmonary resuscitation."

"DNR? My mom had a DNR order?" Julie cried.

"Yes . . . I'm so sorry . . . we did everything we could."

There was no immediate response. Ashley observed each person in the room as each of their faces absorbed the awful truth.

Nancy was dead?

A devastating sob erupted from Christopher. It was the first sound to pierce the silence in the room. He'd said nothing since Dr. Alberty entered. Ashley rushed to his side, wrapping her arms around his shaking body.

"This was supposed to be a routine operation. You said the chances of serious complications were slim. I researched it . . . four in one hundred thousand living organ donors die. Why my mom?" Michael slammed his foot back against the seating. "Why is my mom one of those four?" he yelled. "What did you do wrong? What aren't you telling us?"

Michael was beside himself. Ashley had never seen his calm demeanour so animated. He slammed the palm of his hand against the wall multiple times before dropping to the floor.

"Michael, stop," Julie screamed.

"Mr. Davis, please." Dr. Alberty remained calm; she gestured towards the chair. "Do you mind if I sit?" She didn't give him the chance to respond. She was trained to deal with grieving family members; it was part of the job. "I understand you're upset; you have every right to be angry, but if you will allow me, I can explain." Her tone was lower now, more soothing. She took his silence as an invitation and moved to the seat beside where he was slumped on the floor. She leant forwards slightly. Michael buried his head in his hands, visibly distressed.

"In some rare cases, the anaesthetic can cause a patient to have a stroke during surgery. This isn't something we can predict or prevent from happening. Nancy suffered a stroke, which created a blood clot that cut off the blood supply to her brain and her heart. When the heart doesn't receive oxygen from the blood flow, it begins to die."

Julie stood against the far wall, rooted in place, her eyes squeezed shut. "I thought DNRs didn't apply if you're in surgery?" Julie asked.

"Many physicians do try to have the order suspended in the operating room, and they have it reinstated once the patient is out of the ICU. Ultimately, it is the patient's decision. Nancy was of sound mind, and she chose to keep her DNR order in place. I accepted her wishes."

"Could you have saved her? If there was no DNR?" Julie questioned.

Dr. Alberty walked towards the doorway where Julie stood. She placed a hand on her shoulder and squeezed gently. "Nancy was terminally ill, and although it seems that you've lost her too soon. Her wish for the DNR was to prevent you from having to see her suffer. She didn't want you to have to watch day in day out as she grew weaker. She wanted you to remember her as you've always known her, not how you would've seen her at the end. As hard as it is now, you will one day take some comfort in knowing that she left this earth on her own terms."

She turned back to face the room. "I am so sorry for your loss. I will update you on Megan's condition shortly."

"When can I see my daughter?" Amanda asked.

"As soon as she's stable. I will have someone come and get you when she's back on the ward."

Amanda nodded before turning her attention to her husband. Ashley's heart ached for Michael. His daughter had survived a horrific accident. That would bring him great happiness, but the happiness was fleeting. It was quickly overpowered by the grief of losing his mother.

Julie looked numb; she began searching through her bag looking for her phone. Within minutes she had a funeral director's website on her search engine. Autopilot would get her through the next few weeks. The sadness that came with real loss was too overwhelming for some people.

Christopher trembled beside Ashley. She held back her own tears and pushed aside her own sadness to comfort him.

"I'm so sorry," she whispered.

He reached for her hand, holding it tightly; his hands looked wrinkled and frail. The gold wedding band on his left finger sat tightly against his skin. She often forgot his age; he'd turned eighty earlier that year, but he still walked everywhere, and he worked the odd shift at his bar. Granted, it was more a novelty now than an actual job, but he enjoyed being a part of it.

Ashley recalled a conversation she'd had with Christopher and Nancy earlier that year. They spoke about travelling the country together when they turned eighty. They'd buy an RV and get used to the open road before eventually travelling the world. There was still so much they hadn't experienced together. The notion broke Ashley's heart.

They were childhood sweethearts who'd been torn apart in the height of their love story. They'd been separated for years. They'd lived ordinary lives waiting and hoping they would somehow find their way back together. Eventually they did. They got married. They combined their lives and tried desperately to make up for lost time.

Twenty years seemed like a long time, until it was over. Christopher was left a widower. The dreams of their future, even at eighty years old, were left in ruins. The trauma was too much for Ashley to absorb.

Nancy had been a huge part of her life, from their first meeting until now. Her willingness to share stories about her life, to give the most wonderful advice when it was needed and to offer a helping hand or a hug when her day took an unexpected turn, had been a gift in Ashley's life. Nancy was the perfect role model. Ashley finally let the tears fall knowing that she would miss Nancy forever.

***

The clock struck 7:00 p.m. It was now fifty-four hours post-surgery. Doctors had reversed Megan's medically induced coma, slowly weening her off the drugs whilst monitoring her vital signs. All they could do was wait. Dr. Alberty had given them no specific timeline. "Every patient was different," she'd said. They'd done all they could do. It was up to Megan now.

It had been over a week since she'd last opened her eyes, a week since she'd spoken a word. Ashley had resorted to watching videos of them together just to hear her voice. One night she dove five years deep into Megan's social media profiles with no way out. Each video made her laugh, smile and eventually cry.

That evening in the hospital was no different; the sirens outside indicated the ER was filling up. The corridors grew quieter as the evening stretched on. She had conversations with the nurses as she passed their station. She gave a brief hello to the gentleman across the hall who was waiting for his wife to return from her routine bath. His name was Harry. Ashley saw him twice a day sometimes. His wife seemed to deteriorate daily which filled her with sadness. There was no way they were leaving the hospital together, but for the sake of Harry she pretended anyway.

"Looking good, Harry. How's your wife today?" Ashley raised her hand in a salute. Harry wore a perfectly ironed pair of khaki slacks with a striped grey t-shirt tucked in.

"She's getting there. What about your lady?"

"She's getting there, Harry."

"Good. I'll bet we both get out this week." He grinned.

"I hope so."

"I hope so too."

"Take care, Harry."

He waved. "You too, my dear."

When she walked into Megan's room, the intern finished checking her vitals, but there was nobody else around. "Evening, Ashley."

"Evening. Where's Julie?" Ashley asked.

"She had to leave early today something about a last-minute cancellation."

The funeral director, Ashley thought. "Ah okay. Has anyone been by to visit today?" She knew the schedule, but asked anyway.

"Her parents this afternoon. A younger girl this morning." *Sofia*.

Ashley walked to the opposite side of the bed and took a seat in the blue plastic covered chair she'd become accustomed to. They'd agreed to visit Megan in shifts so that someone would be there when she woke up. When the doctor informed them that it could take a week, they had to be realistic about their commitments. Ashley rode the family emergency card at work for a week before she had to return. Today had been her first day back; so she took the evening shift. Julie could manoeuvre her schedule to a degree. She came in the afternoon. Megan's parents came in the morning, and the rest of the time they helped Christopher begin to adjust.

"Any movement today?" Ashley asked.

"Not yet. But today could be the day." The intern smiled sincerely before turning on his heels and heading for the door.

There was a fresh bunch of flowers added to the window ledge, a bright variety of peach, lilac and pink roses created a delicate display. She reached for the card, it read.

Get well soon, Meg. We can't wait until we're beating your ass on the court again. Sending all the love.
—The Girls xoxo

The New York Liberty had sent gifts, everything from fruit baskets, to jerseys, to the large pink get well soon balloons floating behind Megan's head, and now flowers. That was the thing about Megan, everyone who knew her loved her. The fear of her potentially not being able to play basketball again had crossed Ashley's mind. She tried not to dwell on it, but she knew it would be one of the first questions Megan asked. The chances of a full recovery were good, according to Dr. Alberty, but not guaranteed.

Ashley began telling Megan about her day.

"I went back to work today. I didn't want to, but you know Sonia. Under normal circumstances it would've been a good day. I got offered two tickets to the Knicks game this weekend. I had to decline, obviously, but maybe when you're on your feet again I can ask for some more. Someone bought doughnuts for the break room. There was a pink one with little sprinkles; it was to die for. You know I enjoy it when there are sweet treats involved. I got to see the finished media content for my segment, and the design for the app is so good. I went to call you to tell you all about it, and that's when it hit me . . ." Ashley sighed. "None of it matters without you."

She reached for Megan's hand cradling it delicately in her own. They'd removed the majority of the tubes; only one remained connected through her nose. It was helping her breathe. The machines were quieter, which she took as a good sign. The wound on her head was no longer covered by bandages. All that remained was a thin line. She was lucky, it had been a fairly clean split. The doctor insisted the scar would be barely noticeable. Ashley cringed at the thought of Megan in pain. Her eyes were still bruised, but they had faded to more of a yellow brown. She was starting to look more like Megan again.

"I have spent my whole entire life looking for you. When I met you it was electric. The connection, the bond, it was instant. I figured we'd never find our way back to each other, but we did. You came back to me."

Ashley kissed Megan's hand. The idea of speaking to her whilst she lay there unresponsive felt strange the first time she'd done it. *It's not like she can hear me*, she thought.

"I'm sorry that it took me so long to realise that you were everything I needed. I always knew . . . of course I did. Whether it was a dream, a conversation, a look, or a touch, there were so many unspoken words. There were so many times I forced myself to look the other way, or to ignore the way you made me feel."

She looked at Megan. *How do you still look so perfect?* Ashley wiped at her moist eyes; the puffiness of her cheeks had been a constant feature since the accident. Just when she thought there were no tears left to cry, her eyes filled once again.

"Do you remember when we stayed in the motel on the way to North Carolina? I lay beside you that night and I watched you sleep . . . Now that I've said that out loud it sounds creepy. I promise it wasn't." Her half-hearted chuckle quickly turned into a tight-lipped smile.

"I lay on my back that night, wide awake. You woke up once or twice and I closed my eyes. I never asked if you knew I was awake. I didn't understand my true feelings for you at that point. I was so embarrassed. Now, all I want is for you to wake up and catch me staring at you. I want that more than anything in this world."

Ashley thought she felt Megan's hand twitch. *No, you're imagining things now,* she thought.

"I can't be in this world without you. I know that might sound dramatic and it's probably what most people would say in this situation, but I can't. If you don't wake up, I won't forgive myself. I won't be able to cope with knowing that I knew you for five years before I told you I loved you. I wasted five precious years when I could've been with you. We could've been happy. None of this would've happened if I wasn't so stupid."

She placed Megan's hand gently back on the clinically blue hospital sheets. Ashley buried her head in her hands, trying not to sob. *The doctors will be here soon. Pull yourself together. She's going to wake up.*

She'd said the same thing over and over: on the tube, at work, in the shower, whilst eating, on the rare occasion she could eat. The fact that Megan had been fed through a tube for a week made her feel sick; her guilt was too much to contemplate.

"I just want you to wake up, please, just wake up. Then I can tell you how much I love you."

Ashley felt a soft hand on the side of her face. The unexpected touch caused her body to jolt. Her heart dropped, but she didn't move. She froze in place, her head buried in her hands, unable to look up. A hand, the coolness of fingertips traced behind her ear tucking away her falling strands of hair.

"Tell . . . me . . . then." The words sent a shiver down Ashley's spine. The hairs on her arms stood on end. That voice. She knew that voice. It was slightly hoarser, but she'd waited a week to hear that voice. Her head shot up and she watched as Megan's large green eyes stared back at her. She blinked twice, her mouth gaped as the tears streamed.

"Tell . . . me," Megan repeated.

Ashley stood and leaned over Megan, kissing her head, her cheeks, her lips, her eyes, every part of her face. She felt her lips. "I love you. I love you. I love you so goddamned much."

"I love . . . you . . . too." Megan smiled forcefully, the grimace on her face caused Ashley concern.

"I'll get the doctor."

"No . . . I'm okay . . ." She pointed towards the jug of water on the side table. Ashley remembered the nurse telling her that she could give her water when she woke up because her throat would feel like sandpaper. She obliged, knowing it would help.

"I should get the doctor; they'll want to make sure everything's okay."

Megan reached out her hand, cradling the side of Ashley's face. "Can we just . . . have a minute . . . please?"

She nodded. "We can have all the minutes you want."

"Thank you." Megan touched Ashley's lips with her fingertips. Tracing the edges like she'd never seen them before. "Kiss me."

No sweeter words had ever been said. Ashley obliged again and again. When Megan winced in pain, Ashley knew it was time to call the nurse. Megan's eyes started to scan her body, the casts, the wires, the bruising. Her body was broken, and Ashley observed the look on her face as that realisation sank in. When the nurse arrived, Ashley removed herself from the room to call Megan's parents and Julie.

The future was unknown, Megan's condition, although stable, was still unpredictable. Only time would tell if she would make a full recovery. The fact that she knew who Ashley was and she could speak filled Ashley with confidence. The next few days would be the hardest. Megan waking up had been the focus of the past week, but that was only the first step on a long road to recovery. She would have to process the death of her grandmother and the potential career-ending injuries she'd sustained.

Waking up was just the beginning.

14

Megan

How long have I been asleep? That was her first thought. Along with, *what is that terrible beeping sound?* The heart monitor infuriated her; she made a note to have it switched off immediately. Her mind was clouded with confusion, but she knew where she was. She felt Ashley's presence; she'd heard her speaking, and just when she thought she couldn't respond, her eyes flew open. Megan's vision was unclear, and her muscle movements were tight. Panic set in for a second. She tried to open her mouth. She tried to breathe, but it all felt so foreign. When she caught her first breath, and her vision began to take shape, she looked down and saw Ashley's head buried in the bedsheets. That's when she reached for her.

Small details returned; she remembered the sirens as the ambulance rushed her to the hospital. She remembered the doctors talking over her, debating what to do first, what part of her to *fix*. The conclusion to put her in a medically induced coma had been agreed upon quickly. Despite the fear, she physically could not argue. She remembered being in and out of consciousness; the pain was unbearable at first, but whatever they gave her took all the pain away. She had no recollection of the accident. It all happened in slow motion; she saw headlights and the next thing she saw was the doctor attaching an IV drip to her arm. The rest was a blur.

Ashley had informed her she'd been in a coma for over a week. That had been the biggest shock because to her it felt like a few hours had passed. The only thing she could compare it to was jet lag. After a flight from the US to England she would always sleep longer than necessary. When she woke up her head would feel cloudy, her body weak and her eyes heavy. That was her current feeling. It felt like she'd overslept.

It wasn't until the doctor came that she started to realise the extent of her injuries. The doctor asked her to wiggle her toes and extend her fingers; she could do both with ease which she took as a good sign. Dr. Alberty explained her condition in great detail. She covered what she'd been through and recommended a rehabilitation programme.

The doctor had been there for twenty minutes. Megan barely had time to process the information before her parents arrived. It was overwhelming at first, the way everyone's eyes monitored her every move. She winced and her mother jumped up to get the doctor. They were concerned, which she understood, but all she wanted to do was let out gas, which was embarrassing in itself, and even more so with everyone watching.

"Do you remember anything? I researched a lot about comas. Some people said they could hear everything going on around them," Ashley asked.

"I heard bits, it feels fuzzy now, but I could make out small bits of conversation here and there." She looked towards her father. "Did the Knicks sign Julius Randle?"

Michael laughed. "They did. You remember me telling you?"

"I remember you reading all the headlines to me, but they're all a little mixed up. Kawhi went to the Lakers?" Her eyes widened with optimism.

"You wish, sweetheart. He went to the other team in LA."

"Not the clippers!"

"I'm afraid so."

She lifted her hand and slammed it back on the bed dramatically. "So . . . I almost die . . . and Kawhi can't even help a girl out and trade to the Lakers?"

Her dad quickly stepped to her side and began manoeuvring her wrist. It was flimsy; whichever way he moved it there wasn't much resistance. "Be careful sweetheart, you're pretty weak right now."

"You're weak," she replied.

The room laughed hysterically. The new dose of drugs the nurse had administered made her feel like she was floating on clouds. She liked that feeling. When her dad had finished obsessively checking her limbs as though he was some magical healer, she reached for Ashley's hand.

"I felt you with me."

"You did?"

Megan leant up and nodded before her head flopped back into the pillow. The weight was too much to hold up for a prolonged period.

"I heard you . . . I wanted to hug you." She gulped; the dryness caused her to grimace. "I physically couldn't respond . . . I'm sorry."

"Why are you saying sorry? Are you crazy?" Ashley chuckled through the tears.

Megan gestured for Ashley to come closer. "I'm crazy about you," she whispered.

"Well, that's good to know." Ashley leant forwards and kissed her lips softly. Megan was conscious of her parents trying to pretend they weren't watching her every move, but she'd been asleep for a week. She'd almost died; she figured that was a good enough reason not to care about a little PDA.

"Thank you," Megan said.

"What for?"

"Just being with me. Bringing me the Cronuts." She spied the box on the table to her right. "I could smell them." All she could smell now was a citrusy cleaning solution, *or was it the flowers?* She wasn't sure.

"You could smell them?" Ashley's forehead wrinkled.

"Yes. I can't remember the smell . . . but I remember thinking . . . I would love a bite." Her memory recall was fuzzy. The doctor told her that was normal. There was a moment when all she'd been able to see was black; she hadn't been dreaming, but it felt as though she'd shut her eyes, and no matter how hard she tried she couldn't open them. It had been physically impossible to open her eyes, but she'd heard the conversation, or parts of it. She heard Ashley talking about the Cronuts and that triggered the smell.

"What flavour?" She raised her hand. "Wait, don't tell me." She closed her eyes, trying to remember exactly what she'd heard. "Cranberry?"

Ashley's eyes widened. "They're pumpkin cranberry with nutmeg sugar."

"I love pumpkin cranberry." Megan grinned. That was a lie. She'd never even tried pumpkin cranberry. Although, she really wanted to.

"I don't think they'd be very fresh now, but I can get you some more tomorrow."

"I'd love that."

Ten minutes passed by before Julie came rushing through the doors. Megan noticed her hair was tied back. Unusual, she never tied it back, not unless she was ill, or running. She wore a creased blouse; Julie's clothes were never creased. She insisted on ironing everything she owned. If she didn't do it, the dry-cleaning service in her building did.

"Meg!" She squealed. The tears were instantaneous. She embraced her with the force of a tornado, but Megan didn't have the heart to tell her to stop. "It is so good to see you awake." She felt Julie's hand roam her face, her shoulders, her arms. "Don't you ever do that to me ever again. Or I'll send you on the next flight back to England."

"How is that a punishment?" Michael said confused. "Really that bad living with your parents, huh kiddo?"

"As if, Dad." She gestured towards the water. "Living with you makes me feel good about my jump shot." She winked, or at least she tried. She looked like a glitch in a video game, but the intent was there.

"That's my girl." He grinned.

Julie took a seat at the opposite side to Ashley. When she leant forwards, Megan noticed the necklace around her neck was new. She'd worn the same necklace for as long as Megan could remember, a small solitaire diamond pendant. In its place hung an emerald-green diamond on a thin silver chain. It looked familiar, but Megan couldn't place it.

"Do you remember anything else, sweetheart?" Her mom asked. The way she said it made Megan question what it was they wanted her to remember, or likewise didn't want her to.

"Not much, but I had a really weird dream about Gram."

The atmosphere changed. Megan could sense it.

"Oh really? What happened?" Amanda asked.

"I think it was a dream . . . it was weird, it all kind of felt like a dream, but sometimes it was pitch black and other times I was riding a donkey through the desert or playing basketball with a ten-foot dolphin. So, I'm gunna go ahead and say those bits were the dreams."

The group laughed, but it was forced, as though bad news was coming.

"Was the dolphin good at basketball?" Julie asked.

"Weirdly, yes, he could dunk with his flippers." The image came back to her. "I tried to convince him to sign with the Lakers." She grinned.

"Anyway . . . the Gram thing . . . it was weird." She paused. "First, we had brunch in Central Park; it was a summer day and she wanted to play Frisbee just like we did when I was a kid. Then we went to the Empire State Building, and I asked her, "Gram, why are we here, we've been up here a million times? She said . . ." Megan took another sip of water before continuing. ". . . she said 'When I die, I want you to spread some of my ashes up here.' Then we switched to North Carolina. We were sat in a diner, white booths, I didn't recognise it at first, but I feel like maybe we went there when I was a kid. We had pancakes. Then two old people came to join us . . . Oh God, what were their names . . ." They were on the tip of her tongue.

"Thomas and Susan?" Julie said so softly.

"Yes . . . how did you . . ."

"Just a guess." Her eyes filled up, which Megan found strange. *What's going on?*

"Please, tell us the rest," Julie urged.

"Thomas and Susan seemed to know Gram. They were younger, but they looked older if that makes sense. Anyway, I didn't understand the significance. Gram was excited to see them again though. She said she couldn't wait to move back to North Carolina so they could spend more time together." She watched her dad walk towards the window; he wouldn't look at her which she also found odd.

"There were a few other stops along the way, but they were a little blurry." It was like trying to decipher a videotape when it was being rewound at full speed.

"Then we ended up here. It felt like an out-of-body experience. I was stood watching myself in this bed. Gram was sat there." She pointed to where Julie sat. "She reached for my hand, told me everything would be okay and that she wasn't going to let anything bad happen to me. Then she said 'goodbye' and the doors over there flew open. There was a strong bright light. I remember covering my eyes with my arm and shouting for someone to turn it off. When I opened my eyes she was gone."

Julie lowered her head so Megan could no longer see her eyes, but she saw the tear stains on her trousers, and that was enough. There was an exasperated sigh from her father. Ashley was the only person still looking at Megan, but she too, lost control of her emotions, and her eyes welled up.

"What's going on?" Megan looked back and forth between them. Her gut knew from the moment Julie walked in that something was wrong. She'd assumed Nancy must've been on her way. Then the realisation hit her like a truck on the freeway. Her chest tightened.

"Where's Gram?" Her eyes darted to her mom, who stood silently in the corner. "Please tell me where Gram is? She's coming, right? She has to be coming." Megan pleaded.

"I'm sorry, darling," Amanda said.

"I . . . I don't understand . . . sorry for what?"

"Your gram is gone darling." Julie's grip on her hand tightened.

I'm dreaming. I must be dreaming, she thought. She blinked repeatedly. Nobody disappeared. The room didn't change; four pairs of moist eyes stared back at her.

"I don't believe you." She pulled her hands away. "You're lying."

The room started spinning. Her body felt limp, and her vacant stare looked past her parents and towards the door. She wanted to run, but her broken leg wouldn't allow that. She wished she could make a beeline for the exit, away from the white walls that confined her, away from the reality she couldn't face.

You can't be gone. You can't be.

She blinked, her eyebrows knitted together, her vision blurred and the light in the room became too intense. The heart monitor's beeping faded, and the room went black.

15

Megan

Ashley held Megan's hand tightly. They sat on the front row, the one without kneelers. The area reserved for close family. The unspoken rule for this area: *these are the people that have every right to hyperventilate and grieve uncontrollably.* She hadn't been to church in a long time; she'd forgotten how cold it felt.

The open casket terrified Megan. She'd never seen a dead body, that would be unpleasant on its own, but when that dead body was a family member, someone she'd cherished more than anything, it was almost impossible for her to imagine. She'd decided against viewing Nancy's body the day before.

According to Julie, who'd gone with Christopher to see Nancy, she'd looked peaceful. They'd styled her hair perfectly. She wore her favourite pearl necklace and matching earrings, and they'd tried to position her face so there was a hint of a smile. The thought brought a sadness so deep Megan could barely function. Accepting that Nancy was gone was something she was really struggling with.

Ashley sat to Megan's left and her dad to her right. She could hear the distress of her family. The muted sobbing from Christopher almost jeopardised the anti-emotion wall she'd erected to protect herself. *Stay strong*, she thought.

On the surface Ashley was holding it together well. Every so often she wiped away a solitary tear that rolled down her cheek. Megan could tell that Ashley was trying to stay strong for her, trying to mirror her own emotional state, but she too had known Nancy on a deep level. Nancy had welcomed her into the family with open arms. She knew Ashley loved Nancy like she would've loved her own grandparents. She gripped Ashley's hand tighter. Her presence made things easier.

Funerals were like weddings or milestone birthday parties. Every distant relative was in attendance, a second cousin once removed who'd been absent for two decades, and a best friend from school who insisted on being called Auntie, were just two of the unfamiliar characters.

Megan found the whole thing uncomfortable; she didn't know what to say or how to react. She knew that when the ceremony was over she'd have to stand and allow everyone to pay their respects as they left.

There were only so many times she could hear, "I'm sorry for your loss," before ultimately wishing she could jump in the casket too.

Maybe she was a little cynical. She wanted to say, "Are you sorry though?" to the friend her grandma hadn't seen for thirty years or the hairdresser she used in North Carolina back in the eighties. Maybe it was the guilt talking. Most of them would return home that night, laugh with their families, watch The *Late Late Show* on CBS and go back to normal life.

Maybe that was the problem; she envied their ability to switch off their sadness. She remembered attending the funeral of a boy she went to school with. He was seventeen when he died, and she hadn't seen him for three years. He'd dropped out. Some of her classmates had stayed in contact, but the only interaction she'd had with him was a like on Facebook every six months or so. She went and paid her respects, but she didn't lose sleep over it. She watched his family and his closest friends. They were inconsolable, and she felt for them. She really sympathised with their pain, but that night she went home, she put a pizza in the oven, and she watched the first five episodes of *Gossip Girl*.

She envied other people's ability to switch off. She was fighting desperately to keep it together, and on the inside she was crumbling.

Christopher agreed to do the eulogy. He wiped at his face with a white handkerchief before making his way up to the lectern. He wore a traditional black suit with a white rose pinned to the jacket. The redness around his eyes emphasised his lack of sleep. His face looked drawn as he fumbled to remove the sheets of paper from his pocket.

Megan pulled Ashley's hand closer; their fingers intertwined as she prepared for what was to come.

"I feel like I should start by saying thank you for being here today. Nancy was always a fantastic host, so I feel like I'd be in trouble if I didn't welcome you." Christopher smiled softly.

"How do you compile a lifetime of memories and experiences into a ten-minute eulogy? That is something I struggled with when I began writing this." He composed himself.

"Nancy was truly one of a kind. She was a doting mother, a loving wife and an incredible grandmother. She had this magical way of bringing joy to all those around her. If you were ever having a bad day, just seeing her smile would change your whole outlook on the situation." He paused.

"She had such kind eyes and that laugh. If you were ever in the room when she watched Chris Rock on the TV, you'll know what laugh I mean. It was infectious. Family was the most important thing to Nancy. She adored her family. Her two wonderful children, her granddaughter and Ashley who brought so much joy to her life over the past five years." He looked at Ashley, acknowledging her presence as someone who'd been important in Nancy's life. It was a nice touch.

"I always thought she had a sixth sense. She used to know when I'd forgotten to do something, she'd call me up at the bar and say, 'you didn't pick up the snacks from the supplier did you?' she just knew. Before Megan came back to New York she said, 'Megan's coming back home next year.' She'd always say it. Something told her you were going to come back, and her death was no different." He turned the page.

"She left me numerous letters, one titled: *For My Funeral.* So here goes."

Christopher opened a small envelope and pulled out a single sided piece of paper. He took a deep breath and continued.

"If you're reading this it means you're currently stood in front of a crowd of mourners, and no you're not at the Knicks game. At least I hope you're all mourning, if you're celebrating, I'll haunt you for the rest of your lives." There was a small chuckle from the pews. Even in death she was still trying to make people laugh. *God, I miss you, Gram*, Megan thought.

"I have loved every moment being on this earth. Each one of you has brought something special to my life at one time or another, and for that I am eternally grateful. Please don't be sad because I'm not here. Instead, remember the love, the laughter, the energy and all the incredible memories we created together. Although, I am not here anymore, those memories will live on forever." Christopher wiped tear droplets from the page.

"Dying is a part of life, yes, it's brutally unfair, but it's simply part of the process. Please don't think I lost at life. I'd say living to eighty is a pretty big victory. Wouldn't you? I was unbelievably lucky to have experienced life with the people I love. Isn't that why we're all here?"

Yes, it is, but you're not here anymore, and I miss you deeply, Megan thought.

"From the bottom of my heart I hope you all live long, healthy and happy lives. Enjoy life. Live every day as if it's your last. Be kind. Embrace each other. Be honest and humble and care. Cherish your loved ones, even when you're angry. Lastly, every single day when you wake up and you take that first big breath of air, when you fill your lungs as you lunge out of bed to start your day, remember how lucky you are to experience this world once more. Make it count. Do me proud. I'll see you again soon."

Christopher placed the letter on the top of the casket next to Nancy's photo and returned to finish his eulogy.

"From the moment I set eyes on Nancy I knew she was the one for me. Even at eighteen years of age, she had such poise and grace. Fast forward thirty years and I married her. I remember how beautiful she looked walking down the aisle. I remember feeling like life couldn't get any better. I was lucky to feel that way for a long time. I am a broken man now. My better half is gone, but I see her still in the faces of her children and all around me in everything I do."

Christopher wiped at his eyes, before saying a final goodbye to the late love of his life.

"Nancy, my sweet Nancy, may you be at peace. I will continue to love you in this life until the day I join you in the next. Goodbye for now my love."

16

Ashley
One Month Later

Column 19 (Draft)

Last month I lost someone close to me. Someone who made the world a better place. Before I met Nancy, my inspirations were fleeting, and my reasons for wanting to write were unclear to me. Over the years she helped me see my potential; she believed in my dreams when I didn't. I have struggled with her loss every day since. Things will never be the same for the people who loved her, and that's okay.

I realised recently that it's okay to show emotion. It's okay to feel weak and lost. It hurts, physically, emotionally and spiritually, but the hurt is a gift right now. It is a reminder of just how much her life meant to me.

I miss her smile, her old-fashioned jokes and the way her presence lit up any room. Although she wasn't my family by blood, she was my family by choice.

We are all blessed, blessed because we make the decision to love, even if that makes grief so much harder.

We are all faced with choices, the cause and effect of our lives. Nancy made a choice to put her own life at risk in order to save her granddaughter. It was her choice to make and to her it was the right one. When we're the ones left behind, we too have choices to make. We can choose to shut down or we can keep their spirits alive. Talk about your loved ones often. Discuss the memories you hold dear, and reminisce as often as your body allows.

Grief isn't constant; it'll ebb and flow like the sea. It is important to remember that, even at your worst, when the waves are crashing over you and you feel yourself being pulled under by the sheer force of your grief, remember that it will fade. It always fades.

Next week's column will be a little different from the soppy romance I normally like to shine a light on. I want to hear YOUR stories, your real-life experiences of grief and loss, but also of hope and courage. It is my aim that the stories provided will help us all become a little less isolated in our own grief.

Ashley closed her laptop. Another column done. The next one would be a little different, but it was necessary. She hoped to discuss the subject of pain and how it could be healing. She'd thought about Megan as she wrote it, and hoped that other people's stories would help her in some way.

Since the moment she'd decided to take the leap of faith with Megan and accompany her to England, Ashley's mind had been consumed with thoughts of Megan. As she scouted the apartment for her hairbrush, she came across the bracelet Megan had given her on the day of her wedding. It lay gathering dust in the bowl she and Emily used for keys and anything else small; the contents included her lost earring and over twenty of Emily's hair grips. The bracelet brought a smile to her face.

It had been two weeks since Nancy's funeral and three weeks since Megan had been discharged from hospital. Ashley had temporarily moved into Julie's condo to support Megan with her recovery. The doctor advised 6–8 weeks at least before she would be back on her feet. Ashley had accompanied her to a check-up the day before. The doctor was pleased with her progress. The minor cuts and bruises across Megan's body had healed quickly, but her leg would be in a cast for another six weeks. The kidney transplant was a subject she didn't broach. Megan would entertain the conversation when she saw the doctor, but outside of that environment she preferred not to discuss it.

Megan experienced an emotional rollercoaster daily. Some days all Ashley could do was hold her until the crying stopped. The blame she placed on herself for Nancy's death sent her spiralling into episodes of unbearable grief. The fear of saying or doing the wrong thing remained, but Ashley didn't shy away from supporting Megan in what was undoubtedly the most difficult experience of her life.

The nights were the hardest. Megan's sleep was plagued, night after night, with terrible nightmares. She woke up screaming, sobbing or even worse, having forgotten. Sometimes she forgot that Nancy was dead, or that the accident had happened. Those bouts of forgetting only lasted minutes, and then the realisation would hit her all over again. It was painful to watch; Ashley's heart ached and longed to take away the agony etched on her face.

Later that afternoon, Emily returned home from a weekend away with Sofia. They'd taken a trip to The Hamptons to celebrate their six-month anniversary. She strolled through the door with her handbag on her arm, a pair of outrageously large sunglasses and a new baby-blue tracksuit she'd purchased from the mall in Manhattan.

"Ash, are you home?" she called, sliding her case up against the wall.

"Hi." Ashley eyed her appearance with a smirk. "Where are your friends?"

Emily looked back at the door confused. "What friends?"

"The Vandergelds?"

She pushed her glasses up onto her head. "I don't know what you're talking about."

"You're Brittany Wilson, aren't you?" She chuckled.

Then the penny dropped. "Oh, I hate you." She hit the side of Ashley's body with her weekend bag.

"You're literally dressed like her; you look like her, and you've just come from the Hamptons. I'm waiting for your driver to bring in your Louis Vuitton dog carrier."

She'd been saving the *White Chicks* reference for weeks. It was a film they held dear to their hearts— Madison included.

"You do realise that's not an insult. She's a bad bitch, like me," Emily said, clicking her fingers for extra effect.

Ashley flopped over the arm of the sofa and gestured for Emily to join her, she obliged.

"How was your weekend?" Ashley asked.

"Amazing. Aside from the obvious."

The look on Ashley's face indicated it wasn't obvious to her.

"Did I not tell you?" Emily said, stopping in her attempt to untie her shoelaces.

"No?"

"Oh . . . I told Madison . . . I just assumed . . . Never mind." Ashley knew exactly what she'd done. It wasn't the first time since their break-up that she'd told Madison something and just assumed Madison would tell Ashley.

"We went down to the beach, there was a cute seafood place when we got to Hampton Bays, and I was craving oysters. They'd run out of oysters, so I ordered the shrimp. They came on this nice little wooden board with some shrimp butter sauce, and everything seemed just perfectly tasty and *nice.*" She made a point of emphasising *nice* on the second occasion. "That was until we got back to the hotel later that night. I threw up everywhere . . . and I mean *everywhere.* I know I'm naturally a bit of a drama queen, but the whole scene was so melodramatic I could've been nominated for an Oscar for best food related performance." Emily winning an Oscar. *Stranger things have happened*, Ashley thought.

"Wow." Ashley rolled her eyes. "Do you know how often I've been away and caught food poisoning?"

Emily shook her head.

"Zero times. I've known you for eight years and I can comfortably say there've been at least three occasions."

"Really?" She rejected the statement. "No . . . I don't think so."

"Just last year we went to the Japanese place on the corner of 55th and Lex. You had the dodgy chicken, and you were throwing up all of the next day. Do you remember?"

She grabbed her stomach, squeezing her face tight as she pretended to be in pain. "I was not in a good way."

"No. Neither was I after holding your hair back and cleaning the bathroom five times. Why don't you just try ordering something less likely to be contaminated."

Emily frowned. "I'm not going to the Hamptons and eating lettuce."

Ashley let out a deep breath. "Okay, keep getting food poisoning." Then she remembered Emily's earlier comment. "So, you've been speaking to Madison?"

"Of course."

"How's she doing?"

"Good. She wants to grab dinner tomorrow evening."

Why? There was a pang of jealousy stronger than she'd expected. She couldn't decide if she was being a little possessive of her best friend, or if it was her fear of missing out. They'd been a threesome for so many years. Now that was over, and it was all Ashley's fault. Granted, she'd come to terms with that, and she wanted to make amends. She hadn't said it out loud, but she missed Madison.

"Oh. Where are you going?"

"We haven't decided yet."

"Huh . . ."

"What?" Emily smirked.

"Nothing."

"Ash . . . what is it?"

"I'm a little jealous that you're telling Madison stuff that you're not telling me, okay? . . . sue me." She folded her arms and sulked humorously. The child like behaviour was customary in their relationship.

"You know that I usually tell you everything, but you've got a lot on your plate right now. I don't want to bother you with stories of vomit and piss."

"I love vomit and piss!" She realised what she'd said and grimaced. "Okay . . . I didn't mean that. Wait . . . there's a story about piss?"

Emily leant her head back against the cushions. "The second night I got very drunk, and I took a little tinkle on the floor."

Ashley shot up. "Emily!"

"What? I got to the bathroom; I just missed the toilet." She shrugged.

"How?"

"Two for one cocktails, that's how," she confessed. "That's not even the best part."

Ashley grabbed the cushion and momentarily covered her face with it. Her words came out muffled. "What did you do?"

"I slipped in it." Emily burst out laughing. She stood up and demonstrated her unfortunate fall, the armchair acting as the toilet in her re-enactment. They spent the next thirty seconds laughing uncontrollably.

"You know what? As hilarious as that is, it doesn't even come close to the most embarrassing thing you've ever done; so I wouldn't worry."

"True. Very true."

There was the time she'd screenshotted a conversation with her previous employer's new assistant, and instead of sending it to Ashley, she'd sent it back to said assistant. She'd included the caption *God she's boring* and a sleeping emoji.

There was the time she'd gone on a date whilst on her period and bled through the dress she was wearing. Luckily the dress was black, but the seat covering at the restaurant was cream. She'd left swiftly before the waitress noticed, but she was so embarrassed that she never saw her date again.

Another time, she was flirting with the woman behind the counter at the coffee shop, trying to stall, she began eating what she thought were sample pieces of croissant, but it turned out it was someone's plate they'd returned to the counter. She left and never returned to that coffee shop. The list was endless.

"How's Megan?" Emily asked.

"She's getting there."

"Has she read the letter yet?"

Ashley shook her head. "No, she still won't touch it."

"Why?"

"She just says it doesn't matter what it says because it's not going to bring her back."

The letter, written by Nancy for Megan prior to her passing, lay in Megan's bedside drawer. Ashley tried to get her to read it, but she still couldn't bring herself to acknowledge her grandmother's death, not properly.

"True, but Nancy didn't write it for her not to read it. She obviously hoped it would bring some clarity, or closure or something."

"I know. I said that. I'm sure she will when she's ready."

Emily spied Ashley's hold-all near the door. "When are you heading back?"

"Soon. I had some deadlines to meet, so I wanted the peace and quiet."

"Loud over at the condo of dreams?" Emily raised her eyebrow.

"It is when Megan and Michael are watching basketball. There've been games on all day today."

"Her parents are back then?"

Michael and Amanda had flown back to England a week after the funeral to deal with some business. They planned to be back and forth a lot more than they had in the past. Nancy's death and Megan's accident had highlighted the importance of family during hard times.

"They flew in two days ago."

"Can't you come home then? I miss you." Emily pouted.

"I'm sure Megan wouldn't mind now that her parents are back. She likes me being there, but it is getting a little crowded."

Emily launched herself onto the sofa where Ashley sprawled. "Stay here tonight." She fluttered her eyelids. "Pleaseeeeeeee."

"On one condition . . ."

"Anything," Emily said.

"We watch *Legally Blonde*."

"Deal! You hungry?"

"Starving," Ashley said.

They were long overdue a night of movies and junk food.

***

The next day Ashley made her way back to Julie's apartment. The smell of garlic and herbs engulfed Ashley's senses as she left the elevator. She had a large black hold-all slung over one shoulder and a brown box, slightly larger than a shoe box, in her hand. Megan's mom was a great cook; you could tell she was in town by the smell of the corridor.

She searched for the small gold key that allowed her access to Julie's apartment. On one hand, having a key filled her with the confidence that she belonged. It was proof that Julie, as well as Megan, wanted her to be there. On the other hand, it scared her to death. She was falling more in love with Megan every day. They shared the same deepest longings and were tied together even more strongly through despair and grief. All Ashley wanted to do was know her, hold her, love her and to experience everything the world had to offer with her. Their connection knew no boundaries. Although they built walls intended to block out certain worries, those came crashing down when they were alone. And yet, she still noticed a small, unsettling urge to retreat. *Love is scary.*

"Hi Ashley," Amanda greeted her.

"Hey! Smells amazing in here."

"I'm making fettuccine alfredo, are you hungry? I wasn't sure what time you'd be coming, but I made enough."

Ashley inhaled the rich cheesy sauce coating the pasta. "I skipped lunch. So, yes please, that would be amazing."

Amanda reached for the cheese grater. "No problem. It'll be ready in ten."

"Thank you so much; you're the best."

There was no sign of Michael. Ashley assumed he'd be in the gym or running, and Julie wouldn't arrive home from work until after 7:00 p.m. She made her way to the bedroom at the end of the hall. The door was ajar, and she spotted Megan hopping from the bathroom back to her bed.

"Hey pretty girl." Ashley grinned.

"Hey you."

"You ought to be careful with that leg."

"It's fine." She shrugged.

Ashley dropped her bag at the end of the bed before sliding in next to Megan. Ashley opened her arm wide for Megan to lean in against her chest.

"How was your day?" Ashley asked.

"Oh, you know, the usual. I watched some TV, ate some fruit, tried a little light exercise, upper body of course. My dad took me across to Central Park for some fresh air, which was nice, but then we passed the bench and I . . . I just wanted to come back."

Ashley brushed the hair back from Megan's forehead and kissed it gently. "I understand."

"I'm glad you're back. I missed you last night." Megan looked up.

"You did?"

"Of course! I'm getting used to having your body to snuggle at night. Plus, it helps that you're heated like a radiator." Her arm wrapped around Ashley's torso.

"I see. So, basically, I'm like your human heated blanket?"

"Yes, but it also helps that I find you extremely attractive." She turned, looking directly at Ashley.

"Extremely?"

Megan nodded. "Uh huh." She brushed her mouth against Ashley's. Just the slightest touch sent shivers through her nerves. Ashley decided she could live off the taste of Megan's lips alone, for a lifetime. Their kiss was soft and tender; the passion was there, but the heat that had been present in England had diminished. It would remain alight, like a burning torch in the distance, until Megan made a full recovery.

When Megan pulled away, she gestured towards the drawer in her nightstand. "Will you pass me a hair band please?"

"Sure." Towards the back of the drawer was the letter titled: *My darling Megan.* It was still unopened. Ashley lifted the letter from the bedside drawer. "Are you going to read this?"

"Yes," she said, sounding unsure.

"You can't keep it in there forever, Meg. Don't you want to know what Nancy said?"

"I'm going to read it," she protested. "I just need more time." Megan slid from the bed and reached for her crutches.

"I think it could help you understand, y'know." She slid the drawer closed and handed Megan the hair band.

"I'm going to see if dinners ready." Megan took off towards door.

"Wait." Ashley stood up. "You can't just keep avoiding it Meg."

"Why?"

"It's not healthy. You need to grieve." Ashley reached forward for Megan's hand. She pulled away.

"You keep avoiding it, so why can't I?" Megan bit back.

"I'm not avoiding anything." Ashley said.

"Yes, you are. You're trying to babysit me because you feel guilty. Admit it."

Ashley swallowed hard. "That's not fair."

"I don't need you to feel sorry for me, Ashley. I'm not some charity case."

"Why are you trying to hurt me?" Ashley winced. "All I have done since your accident is be by your side. I have tried to support you through this as best I can, but I can't always be your punching bag."

"I think supporting me is the least you can do." Megan hissed.

"What's that supposed to mean?"

"Nothing." Megan turned to open the door. Ashley reached forward and pushed it back in its frame.

"No, go on. Tell me, what's that supposed to mean, Megan?" She didn't answer. "You think this is all my fault? Just say it. What are you waiting for? Say how you feel."

"Fine. It's your fault." Megan's face instantly dropped.

Ashley's chin started to tremble. "Do you not think I know that? Do you not think I am fully aware that if we'd never have met, or I'd never come to England, or you'd never seen me talking to Madison that night, that we wouldn't be in this position?" Ashley's voice grew louder. "I fucking know, okay? I know it's my fault. I can see it on everyone's face when they talk about Nancy. They try not to say it, but secretly they're blaming me." Ashley slammed her hand against the door, and walked over to collect her bag.

"Ashley. . ." Megan frantically followed her across the room. "What are you doing? Don't leave."

***

Ashley is slumped at the end of Megan's bed. The tears have subsided, but her moist eyes remained red and puffy. The guilt she felt from Nancy's death was evident, but she'd tried so hard to bury it.

"I didn't mean it." Megan whispered. "Ashley. . ." Megan was sitting beside her. She reached over to lift Ashley's chin towards her.

"I'm sorry." Ashley sobbed. "If I could take it all back I would."

"No, you wouldn't." Megan said. "I wouldn't allow you to."

"This isn't about me." She wiped at her eyes aggressively. "I didn't want to make this about my feelings."

"Your feelings are just as important as mine." Megan pushed herself up with her arms into a better seated position. She gasped.

"Are you okay?" Ashley jolted forward.

"I'm fine. Just a twinge." Her right arm was healing, but slowly.

"Are you sure?" Ashley asked.

"Yes. Stop worrying about me."

"I'll always worry about you. I love you."

Megan placed her head on Ashley's shoulder. "I know."

"I loved Nancy." Ashley said.

"I know."

"I would've taken her place if I could. You have to know that. If I had been a match, I would've taken her place in a heartbeat." Ashley pinched the corners of her eyes with her outstretched fingers.

"I don't blame you." Megan sighed. "Nobody blames you. If anything I blame myself."

Ashley shook her head. "No."

"I chose to come to the party. I chose to walk away from the party. We could all find some way to blame ourselves if we wanted to." They both allowed the silence to fill the room for a short moment.

Megan kissed Ashley's cheek and whispered in her ear. "I need you."

"I'm not going anywhere."

"Promise?"

"I promise." Ashley replied.

They were both grieving. They were both hurting. Ashley had tried so hard to be strong for Megan. She tried to pretend that she didn't carry the overbearing guilt with her on a daily basis, but the truth was, she did. She wasn't sure if that would ever go away, but in sharing her feelings with Megan she felt some relief. Maybe she didn't need to be so perfectly supportive all of the time, she too could breakdown, she could make mistakes, and that was okay.

Ashley pulled a small brown box from her bag. The box contained a selection of things from Nancy's house. When Ashley had stopped by a few days earlier to do her regular check on Christopher, he'd been sorting through some old boxes. He'd allowed Ashley to take a few things. There was a photo of Megan and Nancy in the summer of 1999, a birthday card Megan had drawn for Nancy from 2001, and a discoloured silver bracelet with a dolphin charm on it. It was the same one Megan wore in the photo. Ashley hoped the selection of keepsakes would help Megan to reminisce on all the good times.

17

Megan
Six Weeks Later

The Letter.

Megan reached for the box at the bottom of her wardrobe. That's where she kept the things she considered valuable. A thief wouldn't have a hard time finding them, but then again, the chances of a robber making their way past the security outside, the overly observant clerk and the security inside, were slim.

The black shoebox that once housed her Kobe VI special edition sneakers now held a collection of memories: the badge from her first semi-professional jersey, a headband Carmelo Anthony handed her at a Knicks game in 2011, a journal she'd written in high school containing segments from all her friends, a collection of photos of her and Ashley and a personalised keyring from a trip to Disneyland when she was eight. The items in the box didn't hold much value to anyone else. Well, maybe the Carmelo Anthony sweatband, she could sell that on eBay for a few bucks. Aside from that, they were all personal to her. Each item signified a memory, a moment in time when she was at her happiest.

Except for one.

The letter remained on top and unopened. It had made its way from the nightstand to the box to avoid the sinking feeling every time she saw it. She retrieved it and sat back against the wardrobe. The smell had faded. When she had received the letter Nancy's scent could be detected. Megan held the paper to her nose now—nothing.

Just like Nancy, the smell was gone.

She traced the edges of the envelope with her fingers, imagining Nancy writing the contents. Did she cry? Did she pray? Did she write it assuming it was merely a precaution? Her gram had a way of knowing things. Maybe that came with experience and age, but Megan wondered if she gave up. When she found out that Nancy had been ill, it all seemed plausible.

She pulled another smaller envelope and two double-sided pieces of paper from inside the larger envelope. A tear hit the page before she'd finished reading the first line.

My Darling,

If you're reading this, it means I am no longer here. When you wake from your extended sleep you will look around the room and see the faces you love so dearly. You will be happy that you get to walk this planet once more. When the overwhelming sensation of being back in this wonderful place we call Earth subsides, when the hugs and kisses and tears of joy slowly falter, you will ask "Where's Gram?" Only then will you realise the faces of the people you love are tear-stained, and not only with joy because you're well again, but with sorrow for me.

The first thing I will not allow is for you to feel any guilt. This was my choice, and it was the easiest choice I have ever had to make in my eighty years on this earth. You, my sweet girl, will one day understand the love a mother has for her daughter and just as powerfully the love a grandmother has for her granddaughter.

I have lived eighty wonderful years, far exceeding any expectations I set for myself. Last year I was told by the wonderful doctors at Presbyterian Hospital that it would soon be my time to go. I was always going to tell you, when the time was right, but what I didn't want was for you to stall your life based on my fate. I hope you can forgive me for that. Your father will explain more about my condition whenever you decide to ask. So, you see, I made a choice knowing the risks and I want you to know that I 100% stand by my choice.

Right now, I know the sadness you feel is overwhelming, but you will be all right. You're stronger than you know. That reminds me of a little story.

When you were young you lost your favourite stuffed animal in Central Park. It was a red squirrel called Princess Acorn. You named her yourself, of course. You'd had her since you were a baby, and you were absolutely devastated; you cried uncontrollably. You told me you'd never be the same again, not without Princess Acorn, but you were. You found a way to move forwards, and you will again.

I'd like to leave you with some advice, if that's okay. Take it from this old lady, I've seen a thing or two in my time. These are things I want you to really understand, some things my mother told me before she passed and some I picked up myself along the way, but they're all important.

Here we go.

First of all, remember that happiness is in the little things: it's Thanksgiving with your family, it's reading your favourite book on a park bench whilst enjoying the summer sun, it's listening to a song that you've always loved even though you've heard it a million times, it's the practice basketball game with your father, the coffee with your best friend, and the movie with the one you love. Happiness comes from the small things we do every day. Don't take them for granted.

Secondly, if you're ever in doubt, always say YES. Say yes to the spontaneous trips, the last-minute dinner dates and the invitation to an event you had absolutely no intention of being at. Just say yes. Believe me, the moments when you're most anxious to say *yes* turn out to be the most fun. I never wanted to go to my high school reunion, but an old friend convinced me to go at the last minute. My life would've been very different had I said no.

Thirdly, remember that life is wonderful. It's a privilege, but it is unpredictable. There is no promise for tomorrow. There is no guarantee that your life will pan out the way you hope it will, so you must live each day as though it's a gift. You must embrace change, let go of worry and just breathe. I mean it. If something isn't going your way, walk outside, breathe in that cool American air and remember you're here. You're present. You're alive, and that alone means your day is a good day.

Lastly, when you find the one, don't let them go. You'll know when you do. I suspect you maybe already have, but only you know that for sure. Trust me when I say they will make your life richer in every way. There is no greater gift in this life than sharing it with your special person. Saying that, you should never have to compromise yourself to be with someone. They should complement you, but that doesn't mean it will always be easy.

One day you will get married. I won't be there to see it in this life, but don't worry, I'll be watching in the next. Just so you'll feel my presence, I have left a few pieces of jewellery with your father, choose whichever you feel a connection to. I have a feeling I know which one you'll choose. That can be your something old.

Below are the vows I wrote for Christopher at my wedding. You were too young to remember, but you sat beside me whilst I wrote them. It was our monthly "weekend with Gram" and you were sound asleep. That was a moment I cherished.

I love you fiercely with everything I am. I love you enough to believe that we can overcome anything as long as we're together. No length of time or distance will be too much for us to conquer. I believe in you enough to stand by you through the good times and the bad, to have faith that we will prevail and trust in our strength as a couple and our love for one another. I will never give up on us. I will spend the rest of my life being present in the moment with you, being your comrade, your confidant and your best friend. I will forever be in love with you, and from this day forward I want the world to know that I choose you. I will always choose you.

Love fiercely my darling. Then, no matter the outcome, you will live with no regrets. I promise.

I have one other letter for you. Some might call it a little bucket list. You introduced me to the idea, and I was hoping you could continue it for me. Do all the things I never got the chance to do? I'll be with you every step of the way.

Before I go, I want you to know that I am ever so proud of you. I love you darling.

Until we meet again.
Gram.

The second smaller envelope had the title, *Bucket List,* written on the front. Megan clutched the envelopes to her chest. She curled her knees up in a ball and sobbed.

"I will make you proud, Gram. I promise," she whispered.

***

The entrance to the training facility in Brooklyn had been shovelled clear of snow, creating a pathway that any normal person could walk down unhindered. For Megan, trying to manoeuvre the spots of ice and clumps of snow whilst on crutches proved difficult. She made her way inside, one agonising hop at a time. When she reached the double doors to the physical therapy room, it was empty. No surprise there, she thought. The weather would have put other players off coming, but she didn't have that luxury. She was in her prime; the best years of her career should be happening now, and all the hard work and sacrifice meant nothing if she didn't play. The 2020 season was five months away. Time was not on her side.

She dropped her crutches at the door and replaced her brace with her ankle air cast for stretches. Megan's cast had been removed after eight weeks instead of the generally recommended twelve. The hospital replaced the cast with a brace as opposed to another cast. It was the only way to accelerate her rehabilitation. The switch to a brace allowed her to start strengthening the weakened muscles in her leg earlier, while the soft tissue was mobile and flexible. The pain was unbearable at first. They were essentially starting her rehab four weeks earlier than the recommended time, but after a week the pain started to settle.

The gentle strengthening and stretching phase lasted three days before she couldn't take it anymore. The desire to play wouldn't allow her to take it easy. By week ten they'd started light weight distribution back onto her broken leg; that was the hardest part. It was week eleven and she was performing aerobic exercises on a daily basis.

She made her way over to the Wattbike. There was no sign of Joe, the teams physical therapist. Megan had been working with him every day. He worked in tandem with the team's athletic trainer and physicians to collectively put together a rehabilitation programme with the goal of returning Megan to full team training in six months. Megan was hoping to speed up the process by 1–2 months. After being told recovering that quickly was physically impossible, she was even more motivated.

The Wattbike started off each session with a twenty-minute ride. The ability to measure the power output of each leg individually meant that Joe could monitor the improvement of Megan's broken leg in comparison with the other. She set off peddling, the pain in her ankle was minimal. The magnet setting on the bike sat at one. The resistance felt uncomfortable but not unbearable. Joe had recommended four weeks at that level.

You can put it up to two, he doesn't know what you're capable of, she thought.

The self-goading in her head grew louder. After five minutes she upped the magnet setting to two, which intensified the force needed to pedal. She grimaced with each movement forwards and back, her right leg trying desperately to keep up with her left.

This is easy. I can do this, she thought.

Then she clicked the setting to three. Now, it felt as though she was biking uphill. Her body screamed. The harder she pushed, the more her ankle tightened. Oddly, it felt good. Maybe she could push through the discomfort. The sweat began to seep through her base layers. Her body burned. Perspiration formed on her hairline and dripped down her frowning forehead tracing the corners of her eyes below. Suddenly there was a sharp, piercing pain.

All movement stopped.

"Ahhhhhhh," She yelled. "Fuck!" The agony took away any control she had over her right leg. She slipped off the bike and onto the hard rubber floor. The doctor had warned her, if she was to overexert herself she would prolong her recovery. Why didn't she listen? She lay on the floor screaming in agony.

The doors flew open and Joe barged in. "What's going on? Megan, are you okay?" He rushed to her side.

"I did too much," she cried.

"Okay, hold on." Joe helped her up onto the physio table. "Sit back, we need to elevate your leg." He adjusted the seating then ran to his office and returned shortly with an ice pack and some painkillers. "Take these while I strap this to your foot."

Joe's raised eyebrow suggested he wanted an explanation, but he already knew the answer. "You turned up the settings, didn't you?"

"Yep." She covered her eyes with her forearm. "I'm sorry. I wish I hadn't."

"I'm not surprised. God only knows what damage you've done. You could've set yourself back weeks."

"I'm just fed-up Joe." She slammed her arm into the side of the table. "I'm so fed up."

"I know, but you have to trust the programme we've put together. I've done this for almost twenty years, Megan. I have worked with some of the most physically fit athletes around. They had to wait too, take it day by day. You're no different than them. You can't cheat the process."

Joe pointed towards her arm. "You need to be careful with that." Full range of movement for her arm had returned after six weeks. It had been a hairline fracture which was her saving grace; a full break would've involved a much longer recovery. She'd been lucky; she hadn't lost shoulder motion, and the aching and swelling of the first month was the extent of it. "Have you been getting some shots up?"

"A few. It's hard with one leg, but I'm trying."

"And?"

"I shoot like shit now."

Joe chuckled. "I doubt that."

"My best is eight for twenty. I used to shoot eighteen for twenty on a bad day." Joe adjusted the ice pack. The pain had numbed slightly.

"You've been out of action for almost twelve weeks Megan, it's going to take time."

"I just want to dribble; I want to take jump shots. I want to be the basketball player I was, right now, but my body says, *no*." She sighed.

"I know the feeling."

"I'm just scared."

He pulled the exercise ball from behind the table and took a seat. "What scares you?"

Megan wasn't used to opening up to Joe. They'd been working together for three weeks, and he was the kind of physical therapist she needed, stern and honest. He was an ex D1 player. He'd tore his ACL in his second year and never fully recovered. After realising he would never face up against the greats, he decided to study to be a physical therapist.

"That I won't be as good as I was before the accident."

"And what if you're not? Have you thought about that?" There was the honesty.

"I assumed you'd just say, of course you will be." She rolled her eyes.

"I won't ever give an athlete false hope. You must consider all options."

"You don't think I'll recover fully, do you?" Megan's heart sank.

"I never said that, but the reality is, you have to be prepared for if you don't."

She'd never considered what else she would do aside from basketball. "When you train for something your whole life, I guess you don't think about the what ifs."

"That's natural, nobody does. Especially when you're good at it, you assume you'll achieve everything you've dreamed of, and in a perfect world you would."

"But there's no such thing."

"Exactly." Joe adjusted the ice pack on Megan's ankle once more. "You know I had to adapt after my injury, and it was tough. I felt like I was grieving the loss of my former self. I was the star point guard. I was on so many NBA scout lists, and then it all came crashing down." He shrugged as though it meant nothing to him now, but Megan could see the pain in his eyes.

"It's cruel."

"It is, but we move on. Have you thought about coaching?"

Some of the collegiate basketball programmes had women head coaches. The WNBA needed more young and ambitious women coaches. She'd not given it much thought, but it was something she'd considered as an option later in her career when her playing days were over.

"When I retire, yes," Megan said.

"I think you'd make a great coach. You have that natural ability to lead."

"I don't know."

"I've seen you after games with the rookies. You take the time to train people, but you're humble about it. They respect that. You're a team player, Megan, and you have the knowledge."

She smiled. "Thanks Joe." Maybe she would make a good coach. *It had to be rewarding, right?*

"Now, let me see this ankle. We need to see if you've done any damage."

The slightest downward movement caused a sharp jolt up her leg. *That's not good.*

18

Megan
Four Weeks Later

With the start of the WNBA season less than four months away Megan had intensified her workouts. The slight setback on her ankle only added to her original plan by a week. Joe had recently increased the workouts from sixty-minute sessions to ninety minutes. They'd introduced mini squats and slope walking to encourage calf and ankle activity. She felt good. Each day pushed her to her limits. By the end of it she was exhausted.

The Christmas period flew by, as a family they couldn't bring themselves to celebrate without Nancy. A room filled with reluctant smiles and sombre faces didn't make for a jolly festive time. She was yet to open the *bucket list* letter Nancy had left her. Ashley had asked her the reasoning behind her decision, and it was a simple one. She had to be healthy. Whatever was written on the list would require Megan to be in a position to uphold her end of the deal, and she would.

She sat on the edge of the sofa, bending to tie her laces. She could finally wear a pair of sneakers. She wasn't entirely comfortable with walking, but the structure and the normality felt great. The swelling of her ankle was almost non-existent which allowed for the extra movement. She wasn't about to run the full length of the court in a fast-break opportunity, but she could walk and that was progress.

The warmth of Ashley's arms pulled her back as she slipped in behind her, wrapping her legs around Megan's body.

"What are you doing?" Megan chuckled.

Ashley slowly brushed Megan's hair to one side, exposing the left side of her neck. Her lips pressed softly against Megan's bare skin; that was enough to make her wish she didn't have to go to physio.

"You smell really good," Ashley said. The kisses moved upwards, tracing her jawline, then her ear; Megan shivered in response.

"You need to stop, seriously. You're . . ." She rolled her head back.

"I'm what?" Ashley said, her grin mischievous.

"You're . . ." She reached up and whispered in her ear. ". . . turning me on."

Ashley moved her hand down towards the waistband of Megan's shorts, slyly untying the drawstring. She raised her eyebrows suggestively. "Surely, you can be a little late to your session." The soothing sound of her voice coupled with the caressing of her stomach was a combination Megan couldn't resist.

"Maybe I can be a little late."

Just when things were getting heated, her phone rang. It was her agent, Cheryl.

"Ignore it," Ashley whispered.

"She doesn't call unless it's important." Megan pried her lips from Ashley's, her initial greeting flustered.

"Hey Cheryl."

"Are you okay? You sound out of breath."

"Yep, all good. Just working out." She leant forwards, putting some distance between her and Ashley.

"How's the rehab going?"

"Good. It's slow progress, but I'm getting there."

"That's great." Cheryl's voice lacked its usual enthusiasm. There was a moment of silence before she continued. "I'm going to get straight to the point."

Megan gulped. "What do you mean?"

"I have some bad news. The New York Liberty aren't willing to renegotiate your contract for another year."

Her heart sank. "I don't understand. I thought we had a two-year deal?"

"The deal included a buyout clause if you were to get injured or if you didn't fit their team dynamic after the first season."

"Oh. Surely, there's something you can do. Aren't they willing to give me a chance to return?"

"They were . . ."

"What changed?"

"They changed their mind when they read through the doctors notes from your last check-up."

Megan paced back and forth; she didn't understand. Her recovery was on track. As far as she was concerned, she'd be back for the start of the 2020 season.

"Have I missed something? The doctor told me everything was healing nicely."

"I don't doubt that, but the organisation has had to weigh up the long-term odds. You had a kidney transplant, Megan. Even though you can resume a mostly normal life, you still have to take medication, and you must avoid anything that could cause serious infection. On top of that, you broke your ankle and fractured your shooting arm. Even if you fully recover, the chances of all three of those things being 100% healthy again are slim. I know it's cruel. I have been back and forth with them for the past forty-eight hours trying to negotiate a deal, but there is no emotional attachment to this on their end. You know what this industry is like. It's a business first and foremost."

"I can't believe this." The tightening in her stomach made her wince. She couldn't register what she was hearing. "How can they do this to me?" She dropped to the floor by the window. Ashley rushed to kneel by her side.

"I'm so sorry, Meg." Cheryl sighed. "For what it's worth the buyout clause will give you enough money to last until you recover fully. Then you can figure out what's next."

What was next? Was this it for her career? How do you process something like that? Did Joe know? He'd been hinting more and more at the prospect of being a coach, trying to persuade her into thinking it was a good idea. Maybe he knew her recovery was impossible.

"What happens now?" Megan asked.

"I will send over the correspondence. All I need you to do is focus on getting better. Once you're healthy again, we can try and negotiate a new contract."

"With Liberty?" She didn't want to play anywhere other than New York. It was her home.

"Maybe. It's not completely off the table. Although, my advice as your friend would be to tell them to stick it where the sun don't shine. As your agent I will obviously fight for the best deal and give you all the options."

"Thank you."

"I'm sorry it couldn't be better news. I'll call you soon."

"Wait . . . Cheryl."

"Yes?"

"What if I wanted to be a head coach?" The words felt wrong, like she'd already given up hope off the basis of a ten-minute phone conversation, but if Liberty didn't want her, who would? That was her biggest fear now.

"I'd say you have all the makings of a successful coach," she said with utter certainty.

***

Nights were when the reality hurt the worst; Megan's life was dramatically changed. She'd started to leave the blinds open, the floor to ceiling windows allowed for a partial view of New York, and something about the light just made her feel content. The soothing sound of the rain pouring against the window was her favourite. It helped her relax, but sleep? That was a different story.

Her dreams became vividly crucifying; they forced her to replay the accident and her time in the hospital a thousand times over. It was like a song on loop; she couldn't escape the reality of the situation. What hurt the most was knowing she could've prevented it had she just been more careful. Her family stressed that it wasn't her fault, "You weren't to know a maniac would hit you with their car." Or, "You're the victim here, you shouldn't feel guilty," but when it boiled down, who could she blame?

The driver? Ashley? Madison?

Christopher, for not challenging Nancy?

The doctors, for not suggesting another alternative?

She struggled the most, knowing that her family and Ashley had allowed Nancy to proceed with the operation despite the risks. Then she'd realise that none of it mattered. None of it brought her back. So, she would sit and dwell, cry and punish herself until the next distraction, and then she'd repeat the cycle all over again.

Ashley strolled in from the en-suite to the right of the bed where she slept. Her blonde hair was now an ashier blonde. They'd lightened it in a DIY fashion; it had turned out surprisingly well. It was pulled off her face in a messy bun. Megan's old Michael Jordan jersey hung off Ashley's body. The profile of her breast could be seen through the arm hole as she raised her arms above her head to release her hair.

How did she make everything look so sexy? Megan thought.

The simple way she flicked her hair to loosen it or the way she extended her toned arms above her head to pull off the jersey fascinated her.

When Ashley slid into bed beside her, Megan knew the warmth of her body would help her forget her worries; plus, sleeping naked had become her favourite thing in life.

"I've been waiting for you. I'm cold." Megan shivered.

"Your personal heater is here now." Ashley smiled. "Have you spoken to Cheryl today?"

Megan nodded.

"And?"

"Do we have to talk about it?" She snuggled in closer.

"Not if you don't want to."

"I told her I'm taking some time away."

"You did? What does that mean?"

"I need to rethink what it is I want to do. I'm not the type to just quit, but I understand the odds are stacked against me. I don't want to jump into a roll I'm not ready for."

"You mean coaching?"

"Yes. If that's the route I go down; I want to be fully prepared. Cheryl already has assurance that numerous WNBA teams would add me to their roster as an assistant coach."

"That's great!" Ashley said enthusiastically.

"I want to make sure I have the right mindset before I accept something like that. One bad stint and nobody would want me in the future. I have to think of the longevity, which is crazy really. I never thought I'd be considering anything other than basketball at this stage in my life."

"I understand."

It was times like this when she thought about Nancy. *What would Gram say?* It was the first thing she asked herself. The guilt consumed her whenever someone said Nancy's name or a memory of her was brought up in conversation. Whenever Megan laughed, or sang, or danced, or play-fought with Ashley, it reminded her that she was alive, but equally that Nancy wasn't.

"I've been thinking today . . ." Megan sat up and faced Ashley.

"Yeah? About what?"

"The bucket list that my gram left. I think now is the time to open it." The second envelope remained untouched. She'd told herself that what was essentially a list of all the things her dead grandmother never got to do was too sad. It would bring too much pain to read it, but a part of her just didn't want it to be over. The letter was the final correspondence between them. After that, all she'd have were memories. "Whatever is on the list, I want to do it."

"Okay."

"Will you do it with me?"

"Of course," Ashley said confidently.

"I mean really do it . . . If it involves travelling the world for the next six months, will you do it?" Megan knew it was a big ask.

Ashley's eyes widened. Her eyebrows arched. "Is that what you want to do? Travel the world?"

"I don't know . . . I have no idea what's on that list, but . . ." Megan paused to gather her emotions. "I want to do it justice. I feel like I owe her that, y'know?"

"Okay."

"I don't want to say I'll get around to it because that's what everyone says. It's never the right time, but now is as good a time as any. I have no commitments. I know that's different for you though; you love your job."

"I do." Ashley reached out to brush Megan's chin with the tip of her thumb. She leaned in and kissed her softly. "But . . . I love you more."

Megan shot back. "So . . ."

"If Nancy wants us to travel the world, then that's exactly what we'll do."

"Seriously?" She gripped either side of Ashley's face; her body felt electric for the first time in weeks. "Even if it's as far as Australia?"

"If you're going to Australia, I'm going to Australia." Ashley grinned, her face squished between Megan's hands. Their conversation was hypothetical at that point, but the gesture made Megan's heart skip a beat. She loved Ashley, beyond measure, beyond reason, beyond doubt; she loved her like she would never love again.

"I love you. I love you. I love you." Megan showered her with kisses and then made a beeline for the wardrobe. "I'll get the letter."

***

The Bucket List.

A must-do itinerary of things you want to do, goals you want to achieve and dreams you want to fulfil before you die. Typically, such a list involved flying across the world or experiencing high-adrenaline pastimes like swimming with sharks or bungee jumping. Thankfully, neither were on the list. Sharks were not a species Megan wanted to get up close and personal with.

Megan had introduced Nancy to the list idea many years prior. It was her way of telling her gram to get out there and enjoy the latter years of her life, years without young children, the responsibility of bills and work—although Nancy preferred to work shifts at the bar to *stay young*.

Megan's list contained many things she hoped to one day achieve and some things that would need to be removed or altered i.e., winning an WNBA championship might now include a side note *as a coach*—that was life.

The idea of valuing *experiences over things* had been drilled into Megan from a young age. She was fortunate enough to have a family that was successful in their own right, and that privilege allowed her to experience some of the nicer things in life, but it hadn't stopped her parents from keeping her grounded. They didn't bombard her with expensive gifts. Instead, they spent money on bonding trips, flights to see family and college tuition. Everything her parents had given her provided something fulfilling, and for that she was grateful.

Megan unfolded the paper, it read, *don't get so caught up in life and responsibilities that you truly forget to live.*

The list.

- **A photography class**
- **Join a march for something important**
- **Scuba dive**
- **Trek The Inca Trail in South America**
- **Visit Machu Picchu**
- **Conquer your biggest fear**
- **Get a tattoo**
- **Go on a safari**
- **Watch tennis at Wimbledon**
- **Learn how to make wine**
- **Adopt a pet**
- **Eat at Pujol in Mexico City**
- **Read *In Search of Lost Time* by Proust**
- **Travel France**
- **Stay in an underwater hotel room**
- **Run/Walk a marathon for charity**
- **Stand on an active volcano**
- **Go truffle hunting in Oregon**
- **Take a cooking class in Italy**
- **Have your portrait painted**

Megan turned the page to find one more.

This one is important. I want you to finish visiting the most iconic landmarks in history. I saw the Colosseum in Italy, Chichen Itza in Mexico and Petra in Jordan on my travels with Christopher. There are four left that I never got the chance to experience. That brings me to the last entry on the bucket list.

- **Visit all seven wonders of the world**

Nancy's list came with a hefty cost, but she had that covered.

I gave your father the details of a gentleman who is desperate to purchase my Nancy Drew collection. That money is yours whenever you're ready. It will be enough to do all the things on this list and more, so don't hesitate. I've given your father specific instructions. That money is not to be spent on material things. Trust an old woman when she says they mean nothing. When it comes to the end, you don't treasure the Prada bag you purchased or the fancy car on your driveway. You treasure the memories you made and the people you made them with.

The greatest gift I can give you is the chance to make a thousand more memories and hope that you do the same with your children one day.

Go and explore.

And no skipping! Gram wants to see EVERYTHING on the list!

Ashley peered over her shoulder as Megan read the list a second time.

"Nance was adventurous." Ashley sounded surprised.

"I feel like she added a few on for my benefit. There is no way my gram wanted to get a tattoo."

"Are you sure about that? I could see Nancy with some barbed wire across her face."

Megan scoffed. "Oh yeah, she was dead set on styling herself after Post Malone."

"Could you imagine?" Ashley laughed.

"It'd be like Meryl Streep getting a skull tattooed on her face." The image was comical. Megan chuckled through the tears.

Ashley climbed in front of Megan. She was, balancing unsteady on her knees with the movement of the bed. Ashley held either side of Megan's shoulders to balance herself.

"Where do we start?" Ashley grinned.

"That depends on what length of sabbatical you can negotiate with work."

"I'll find out tomorrow."

"Are we really doing this?" Megan asked.

"You're damn right we are . . ." Ashley smiled. ". . . for Nancy?"

"For Nancy," Megan agreed.

Megan knew the grief would never go away, not fully. Even in that moment of pure excitement and future plans, she felt sadness in knowing Nancy never got the opportunity to feel that same excitement. Eventually, she would go from thinking about Nancy all the time, to sometimes. She would go from crying every day, to crying once a month. In time she would be able to accept the loss and learn to create a new normal. At least that's what her aunt Julie told her. Having a therapist in the family had its pros and cons— discussing her feelings became part and parcel of being a Davis.

19

Ashley
2 weeks later–Peru

The seven wonders of the world.

The Taj Mahal in India, Christ the Redeemer in Rio de Janeiro, Machu Picchu in Peru and The Great Wall of China all remained on Nancy's list. Peru was where they began. Ashley had convinced Sonia to allow her six months unpaid leave. The conversation had gone surprisingly well. Sonia promised they would use the next two months' worth of stories that Ashley had already prepared as a requirement and then revive her column on her return. It seemed too good to be true, but Sonia made it clear it was a once in a lifetime pass. It wasn't like Ashley could afford to take six months off every few years, so that wasn't a problem.

Megan finished her last physio session on the Tuesday, and they flew out to Peru on Wednesday. Megan had been given the all clear to travel. The doctor did advise saving her *marathon for charity* until the end of their six month trip; her ankle needed time to return to full strength.

Ashley arrived on the ground at Jorge Chàvez International Airport with her nylon backpack and a rough itinerary. She'd agreed with Megan that they wouldn't plan the finer details; they knew what they wanted to see and experience, but the fun would come with the unknown. The flight from New York to Peru was just over seven hours. From there, they boarded another flight to Puerto Maldonado. The second airport was so small that the length of the runway looked like a parking space for a single car. Ashley had to grip the armrests tightly on the bumpy landing, but they made it with the wheels on and the plane intact.

Ashley was hit immediately by the heat when she exited the aircraft. It was eighty-five degrees Fahrenheit. According to the captain, that was mild. The humidity and the lack of air-conditioning made Ashley thankful for the vest she'd put on underneath her hoody.

"Why did you wear a hoody? I told you that you'd be too hot." Megan said matter-of-factly.

"You didn't mind so much when you used it as a pillow on the plane though, did you?" Ashley smirked.

They hopped on the bus with a guide who would take them deep into the jungle. The drive to the dock was approximately an hour. Megan gripped Ashley's hand when she spotted the police escort guiding the bus to its destination. It was unnerving, and the obscene amount of Googling Megan had done the night before hadn't helped the situation.

"It says here that the country is known for petty crime. It says there are gangs! And they strangle and mug you!" Ashley pointed out that according to Google, Peru was no less safe than any other major city in the world, and the chance of being choked until you're unconscious and robbed of your belongings was slim—that's what she hoped anyway.

The long blue boat looked like a giant canoe. They were told when boarding to be careful when moving because the boat had to be balanced out. The large man ahead of them rocked the boat in excitement, undecided on which side he should sit.

The guide yelled, "NO! Stay still!" from the rear of the boat. For several minutes afterwards security and the guides stared him down.

The boat ride was peaceful. Ashley enjoyed the movement of the water. It took just over an hour to reach the lodge they'd be staying in for three nights. The walk to the lodge took just over fifteen minutes. When they arrived, they were given a safety briefing by the guide before being escorted to their room. The lodge was completely handmade; large bamboo sticks were used to create walls. The rooms had mahogany wood flooring with beds to match. The sides of the rooms were open to the rainforest. It was quite the contrast to Ashley's American apartment. There were no windows, only netting that you could partially pull across the open space to keep the bugs out. Ashley listened to the rain falling heavily on the trees beyond the net windows. The sound reminded her of Megan's Spotify playlist back home. They'd stepped into the real-life version of *Rainforest Sounds to Help You Sleep*.

The beds had canopies above them draped in linen bedsheets. The guide nodded towards them saying, "to keep the spiders from falling on you." He winked, before pointing to the safe. "Keep any food in there. You don't want to attract any unwanted animals."

"What kind of unwanted animals might we attract?" Megan gulped.

"Mainly opossums, sometimes monkeys, and very rarely a jaguar."

"He means the car, right? Not the giant cats that will potentially eat me alive." Megan turned to Ashley.

The guide, aka Fernando, shook his head. "Jaguars avoid humans."

"Oh, okay." Ashley breathed a sigh of relief.

"But the bullet ant . . ." Fernando continued.

"Bullet what?" Megan watched the guide walk to the opening that should've housed a window and point towards the wood at the base of the lodge.

"Come here." They rushed over. "You see that?"

"That thing? It looks like a spider. It's huge." Ashley said.

"That's a bullet ant. When they sting, it hurts. Intense throbbing. Like having a nail stuck in your hand."

The ant was roughly one inch in length, with six legs and a large rear end. Ashley didn't like their proximity to the room.

"Will it poison us?" Megan asked.

"The venom is really painful for a period of twenty-four hours, but after that you'll be okay."

"Oh, well that's fine then, sting away." Megan laughed nervously.

Fernando pointed towards the door. "Turn left, head to the bottom and left again, and you will find toilets. Lights out at 10:00 p.m. Please try to be respectful of other guests; these walls are thin. I will see you at 4:00 a.m."

The walls being thin wasn't the problem, Ashley thought. The issue was that the walls didn't reach the roof of the lodge. So, anyone could peer over. Privacy wasn't something they were going to get on this part of their trip.

Ashley freshened up before climbing into bed; She was grateful for the comfortable mattress. She'd half expected it to be like sleeping on a slab of concrete; so she was pleasantly surprised. A concert of humming, buzzing and chirping filled the space around them. The guide had informed them that over twenty-five hundred different species lived in the Amazon. A loud piercing cry ripped through the lodge like an air raid siren.

Ashley froze. "What the hell was that?"

"I think that's a howler monkey." Megan listened. The noise repeated once, twice, three times.

"Yep, I watched a programme on National Geographic. Sounds like them."

"Should I be concerned?" Ashley pulled the sheet further up her body, hiding beneath the crinkled layer of material separating her from potentially a million other creatures.

"I don't think so." Megan snuggled into her chest. "Do you know what I did see though?"

"Oh God."

"The opossums he mentioned. Well, they look a bit like rats. On the programme I watched, a giant spider got hold of one and you could see it dragging it across the forest."

Ashley shivered. "You know I hate spiders."

"Yeah, but this one was so big you couldn't really call it a spider."

"Is that supposed to make me feel better?" Ashley whispered. "You know what I'm struggling with? This wasn't even part of Nancy's list. We opted to do this, by choice. Why did we do that?"

"I'm not entirely sure, but if we don't die it'll be a great story to tell." Megan teased. She wrapped her limbs around Ashley so she felt cocooned. "Your girl will protect you." Megan winked.

The lights went out, and they were left with a flashlight and the promise that the guide was *pretty confident nothing would get into their room,* whatever that meant.

It was going to be a long night. *Unless.* Ashley turned the flashlight towards her face and wiggled her eyebrows suggestively. There was one thing that could take her mind off the potential insect invasion.

"I know that look. Are you crazy?" Megan whispered.

Ashley grinned and angled her body to run her fingers across Megan's bare chest.

"They'll literally here us." Megan pointed frantically behind her to where nothing more than a large wooden partition and a net separated them from the next room.

"Then bite your lip." Ashley pressed her teeth into either side of Megan's earlobe, biting down on the soft fleshy skin.

"Oww," Megan shrieked.

"Ssshhh." Ashley placed her finger to Megan's lips, holding back the laughter. "Sorry."

"I didn't say I didn't like it." Megan arched her neck again allowing Ashley back in.

"Do you think you can be quiet this time?" Ashley teased, running her hand from Megan's chest down to a different region all together.

"That depends . . ." Megan gasped.

"On what?"

"How much you pleasure me."

"Is that a challenge?" Ashley hovered over Megan, bending to kiss and caress the parts of her body that Ashley knew would get her the most aroused.

"Maybe." Megan ran her nails down the sides of Ashley's arms, the added pressure building excitement.

"Challenge accepted." Ashley grinned.

***

The three days passed as fast as the piranhas in the water around the boat. Adventure trips took up the majority of their mornings. During the middle of the day when the sun was at its warmest, they lounged around the lodge, eating, drinking and taking three showers a day. Neither of them complained about that; the showers were more private than the bedrooms, so Ashley enjoyed the alone time with Megan.

They strolled along the jungle trails during the day and once at night—that experience was one they opted out of on the second night. The chances of stepping on a snake or having a spider drop on your head were just too high. Whether it was monkeys, parrots or alligators; there were an abundance of wildlife on the trails.

They took an Amazon River cruise on the second day in search of giant river otters. They found themselves kayaking alongside pink river dolphins and fishing for piranhas—after seeing the film *Piranha 3D* they expected far worse than the little fish on the end of the line with razor-sharp teeth.

According to the guide, like bears and sharks and most other scary things, they will leave you alone if you leave them alone. Ashley wasn't sure she'd categorise baiting them with meat and catching them with a hook through their mouths as leaving them alone, but she didn't dwell too much.

On the final day they strolled through the treetops on the canopy walkways. The excursion took them to a vantage point thirty-five metres up in the trees with a view spanning five hundred metres around the jungle. The experience of being on eye level with hundreds of species of birds whilst being suspended high above ground was a picture to be captured.

"This is incredible." Ashley expressed.

Megan pointed towards a bird in the distance. "Look at how beautiful that is." She reached for the binoculars around Ashley's neck, almost strangling Ashley in the process. "Wow . . .Look, it's so pretty."

Ashley focused in on the blue and yellow bird. "It looks like a Parrot."

"I wonder if it talks." Megan said.

The walkway was enclosed in netting. Ashley grabbed tightly as the suspended walkway moved from side to side. Another member of the group shot from one side to the next to witness something in the trees.

"I think it does. It's looking back at you and saying, 'Gawd ain't she pwetty'."

"In that voice?" Megan chuckled. "You sound like Bugs Bunny."

"That's what I imagine a parrot to sound like." Ashley shrugged.

The guide informed them that it was a blue and yellow Macaw. "If you look closely you'll see part of its face has no feathers, so they blush when they get excited." The guide added.

"That is so cute!" Megan expressed. "My aim in life is now to make a Macaw blush."

"If they like attractive brunette's, then you'll have no problems." Ashley winked.

"Stop." Megan replied shyly.

Ashley set off walking, reaching her hand behind to hold Megan's. She never thought she would take pleasure in bird watching, but anything that involved Megan became undeniably enjoyable.

Aside from the need to lather up with insect repellent five times a day and drink more water than her body could consume, their time in the Amazon was incredible.

The next stop was Machu Picchu. The journey there required a taxi, a plane, a bus and finally a train to get them to the train station known as KM 104. It was the first thing they would be able to cross off Nancy's list. The pictures looked incredible, but nothing compared to being there. After some debate they opted for the one-day Inca Trail option as opposed to the four-day trip. Megan's ankle wasn't in good enough shape to trek over twenty-five miles. The one-day trail was a four-hour trek to the summit, and that would be plenty.

When they reached the peak, seven thousand feet above sea level, the panoramic views took Ashley's breath away. The dry stone wall remains were incredibly well preserved. It wasn't long before the rain started. The fog rolled in, and the conditions became less desirable. They considered heading down the mountain like many other travellers. Instead, Megan pulled Ashley into one of the many old ruins, it was shaped like an old doorway, and it provided the perfect cover. They stood underneath the rocks for an hour watching the rain drive away the travellers, one by one.

It got to 1:00 p.m. and the rain stopped. For the next hour they had the place practically to themselves. Ashley snapped several pictures; they walked in and out of the moss-covered ruins trying to imagine what each room or building had once been in the ancient civilisation that was Machu Picchu.

Megan reached for the small keepsake urn in her backpack. "Shall I spread some here?"

Ashley nodded. Megan had been insistent on taking a small amount of Nancy's ashes on their travels. In each of her bucket list locations Megan intended to leave a little bit of her gram. She removed the lid and slowly shook the jar until a sprinkling got swept away with the wind, dusting the ancient ruins beneath. Ashley found it hard to believe that the small grey speckles of ash once formed the body of a human they'd loved so dearly.

"We can now say a part of her lies upon one of the seven wonders of the world. How cool is that?" Ashley said.

"It's so cool. She'd be happy, right?"

"I'm sure she's up there now grinning from ear to ear." Ashley smiled.

"I think so too," Megan said.

After a moment of reflection, they turned to face each other, snapped a quick picture of them kissing with the incredibly green forest background and took off down the mountain. Another day, another adventure.

**

The flight from Peru to Brazil took five hours. A quick internet search and they found a hotel near the statue of Christ the Redeemer. The hotel had a swimming pool, a necessity in the present heatwave. Trekking around Peru had taken its toll on Megan's foot, so they spent an extra two days lounging around the pool before they finally made the trip to the well-known landmark on Nancy's list.

Ashley had seen pictures on the internet, but she'd completely underestimated the statue's sheer size.

"It's ninety-eight feet tall," Megan said as she stood with her neck cranked upwards and her mouth gaping wide. "How insane is that? Like how did they even put that together?"

A short bearded man took it upon himself to answer the question in passing. "The majority of it was made in Paris in the 1920s; they then shipped it in large pieces here and took it up the mountain via rail to put it together. Amazing, isn't it?" He sounded like a guidebook as he moved his way around the base. They could hear his high-pitched voice spewing facts at all the tourists as he went.

"He's cute." Ashley chuckled.

"Do you know it's only the fourth largest statue of Jesus?" Megan said.

"What? But it's huge."

Megan handed over the brochure she'd purchased on the way up. "There see, there's a bigger one in Bolivia."

"It's 112 feet tall! Wow, people really like this guy, huh?"

"Yeah, I think he's a pretty big deal." Megan smirked.

They took pictures of each other with their arms outstretched beneath the statue, replicating its iconic look. Megan released a small part of Nancy's ashes at the foot of Jesus. Nancy had been brought up in a heavily religious household, so they knew that would mean a lot to her. Just over a week into their trip they'd already ticked three things off the bucket list. Each time they did, it felt like they were getting closer to saying goodbye.

20

Megan
4 weeks later–India

They'd arrived in India two days prior, opting to stay in a more lavish hotel in New Delhi, after backpacking through France and Italy. Adapting to the Indian sun was proving difficult. It was coming to the end of March, and they were about to hit India's summer. Megan was an early riser; she'd been taught at a young age that, *to be successful you need to make sure you're awake when everyone else is asleep.* That's what her dad used to tell her. She used the control system on the in-room iPad to open the shutters. She'd expected some breeze, but already the air was humid, and within seconds her forehead was damp.

The hotel had an open floorplan and screamed contemporary. It had large concrete spaces and spiralling corridors finished off with wooden elements and warm lighting. The large circular doorways created a tunnel through the hotel. There were small speakers on the walls playing music, peaceful and soothing.

The hotel was built on eight acres of impressive gardens. It housed the largest swimming pool in the whole of New Delhi and a spa that they had yet to experience. The signature massage involving Swedish, aromatherapy and a Thai massage was on Megan's personal to-do list.

They'd decided to capture the trip in a journal, making sure to leave space to add photos when they returned home. Megan liked to scribble her entries first thing in the morning whilst Ashley was sleeping. Each time she would read back through the last few pages to refresh her memory.

They'd spent a week in South Africa at the Marataba Safari Lodge enjoying one of the most game-rich and beautiful areas of Waterberg. The healthy population of big cats, rhinos and elephants made for the perfect trips out into the bush. Megan even managed to get a snap of the white rhino that she'd nicknamed *concrete*. Ashley found the whole thing hilarious and still teased her weeks later about her best friend *concrete*. Granted, it was a stupid name, but it was the first thing she'd thought of when she saw its grey scaley skin up close.

France had been the next stop. Nancy had included reading, *In Search of Lost Time,* by Marcel Proust, on her bucket list. Little did they know that the book was 4215 pages long. There were seven volumes in total. By the end of their two-week trip around France they'd only read two thousand pages. The novel, according to many, was recognised as one of the greatest of all time. The story was one very long recollection of the narrator's experiences growing up in high-society France in the early twentieth century.

The more they read, the more they realised the book was about finding your own identity and searching for the meaning of life. Megan was pleasantly surprised.

They explored the history in Lyon, walked the Palace of Versailles, dined with the posh in the French Riviera and visited the Louvre, where they saw *The Mona Lisa*. In reality, it was a painting of a plain woman with an enigmatic expression, but it was a must-see.

Megan admired Ashley's conviction as she took the time to explore the masterpieces of the European Renaissance whilst Megan just rushed straight by to the only portrait she knew. The brochure estimated *The Mona Lisa's* current value in excess of 850 million. The souvenir notebook Megan purchased from the gift shop, with the picture printed on it, was the closest she was going to get to owning anything of that stature.

They left the sweet-smelling *patisseries* of France behind for Italy. First they spent three days in Rome. The ease of the hop on hop off tourist bus allowed them to capture all the main attractions, including the Colosseum—although Nancy had already seen it; Megan couldn't resist.

A cooking class in Tuscany saw them making pasta from scratch. Tiramisu and fettuccini were the dishes of choice. Italy was also the perfect opportunity for them to visit an active volcano; they experienced Mount Vesuvius and the ruins of Pompei. Peering over into the volcanic crater Megan scattered more of Nancy's ashes.

Just reading back through everything they'd already done gave Megan a real sense of achievement. She placed her foot up on the round cushioned footstool; the tingling sensation in her ankle subsided. The six weeks of travelling had involved an obscene number of walked miles. She'd been documenting her daily distance in the journal out of curiosity. One day in Italy they'd done eighteen miles. It had been days and her ankle had barely recovered. The needed relaxation breaks between countries gave her time to recover before the next adventure.

At first, she felt like a burden, when she would ask Ashley to slow down, or to take a short break. Ashley always obliged, she supported her so kindly, but it didn't take away the hopelessness she felt when she couldn't do something. Before the accident she would've beat anyone to the top of a mountain. She'd have taken the steps up to Christ the Redeemer two at a time without breaking a sweat.

She was now brutally aware of her reality—the Megan from before the accident was gone.

Ashley's phone began buzzing on the nightstand. Megan jumped up, trying not to wake her as she reached for the phone and returned to her position outside on the balcony. The buzzing was a video call from Jason. The screen flashed and he appeared.

"Damn girl . . . look at you!"

Megan blushed instantly. "Stop it," she said bashfully.

"Seriously, turn your head; let me see that sun bounce off those glowing cheeks."

She turned her head towards the rising sun whilst pulling what she would categorise as her "cute face".

"This travelling is working wonders for you girl. The bronze sun-kissed skin suits you." Jason knew how to make anyone feel good about themselves. He was a real ego-boost type of friend, and she loved that about him—everyone needed one.

"I just love you," Megan confessed.

"I'm only telling the truth. Where's my best friend anyway?"

"She's sleeping. We had a late night last night. What time is it there?" New York was behind India, but the exact time difference eluded her.

"It's 10:30 p.m. here."

"So, that makes us ten hours in front then."

Jason looked off mysteriously into the distance. "Is there anything I should know about that might be happening tomorrow? Fancy giving me the heads up? Seeing as you're in the future."

"I don't think it works like that." Megan laughed.

"Be cool if it did though. Where's the next stop after India?" Jason asked.

"I can't tell you. It's going to make you jealous, and I don't think I can do that to you." Megan covered her eyes with her free hand, peering through her fingers to see his eyes sharpen; the cogs where turning.

"Oh hell no. If you're going where I think you're going then we can't be friends anymore. That's it, done, *finito*." He flicked back the solitary braid that dangled over his right eye dramatically. The change in hairstyle, according to Jason, added extra versatility to his style and wardrobe. The last time they'd video called, they had to endure a ten-minute chat about the numerous ways he could now wear his braids. Today he'd gone for the man bun, but with one solo braid at the front. Megan didn't say anything.

"You're going to the Maldives, aren't you?"

"No . . ." She averted her eyes from the camera.

"I hate you. Tell Ash, I hate her too." He pouted. "I should have been born in the Maldives. Did I tell you about the time I matched with a cute Maldivian man on a dating site, and we spoke for weeks. Turns out he was only half Maldivian and none of his relatives lived there anymore. Needless to say, we stopped talking. He had the bone structure of a god and incredibly smooth skin, but he worked in finance, and other than the Maldivian heritage he really wasn't that interesting."

"Poor guy." Megan chuckled. "How's things with Louis." Louis was the latest in a long line of Jason's love interests. They'd been dating for three months.

"We're good. That's why I was calling actually; I have some gossip."

"Oh no." Whenever Jason had gossip worthy of a phone call, it was juicy.

"Well, Louis spoke to his friend Jessica, who works with a guy called Liam, who knows Georgina."

"Georgina, as in the girl that Ashley used to date?"

"Uh huh, the one we all couldn't stand because she was a self-obsessed sociopath," Jason clarified. "Apparently Georgina told him she'd had sex with a girl she shouldn't have had sex with."

Megan's eyes widened. "Oh no, not Emily?"

"God no. Emily isn't that stupid. However, you're pretty warm."

"Not Madison?" Megan inhaled.

Jason nodded. "Can you believe it? I haven't had time to clarify her side of the story yet because she didn't answer my call earlier."

"When did this happen?"

"Well, Jessica told Louis last week some time."

"Do you think she's done it to get back at Ashley?"

"I don't know; she's never been the vindictive type. I think it was more than likely a drunken mistake. Georgina is a regular at the bar where Madison works, so they see each other often."

"Interesting." Megan didn't know Georgina. She only knew what the others had told her. Jason probably expected a bigger reaction.

"Does Emily know? Where is she?" Jason was staying with Emily whilst Ashley was away to keep her company. The timing of their travels had given him a few months to figure out his next move. Sofia stayed with Emily occasionally, but they were taking things at a steady pace. Emily worked long hours during the week, so they mostly saw each other on the weekends.

"She's at some networking event for work tonight." Jason shrugged. "But she will 100% freak out when she finds out."

"Are you two getting along? Living together I mean?"

"Sure, apart from the fact she leaves toothpaste all around the sink, doesn't clean her dishes and always loses the remote, everything's fine." He raised his finger and touched it to the tip of his chin. "Actually, she also leaves her clothes in the living room, like who does that? Who gets home from work, takes off half of their clothes in the living area and then practically undresses herself on the way to the shower? I found her bra hanging off the fig tree in the hall yesterday."

Megan burst out laughing. "Did Ashley not warn you of that? I remember her telling me she found her t-shirt in the freezer once."

"The freezer?" Jason nearly choked on his drink.

"Apparently it was during a heatwave a few years back. She was using a bag of frozen vegetables to cool her body, so she put the t-shirt in the freezer with the vegetables." Megan chuckled.

"I love that girl. So, listen if you and Ashley want to move in together when you get back, you just let me know before and I'll take over the lease because I LOVE it here." He exaggerated his tongue movement, highlighting the love part with conviction.

"Oh really?" Megan smirked.

"Any plans for that, or?" He side-eyed her through the camera. There had been a brief conversation about them potentially getting their own place. In reality, they'd only been together for five months. Did it feel too soon? Megan often asked herself, not in the slightest.

"We may have discussed it," she replied sheepishly.

"Okay, that sounds promising." He smirked.

"What about you and Louis though? Don't you want to get your own place?"

He shook his head furiously. "I'm more of a try before you commit type person. I haven't tried enough yet. Basically, he's like a rental car, I'm not sure if I want to commit to purchasing in full yet. So, I'm just paying monthly and seeing how it goes."

"I see." Megan chuckled. "Making sure it drives the way you want it to and checking for dents, etc?"

"Exactly!" Jason heard the door slam; Emily was home. The call abruptly came to an end, the urge to gossip taking over.

Megan felt excited at the prospect of living with Ashley, so excited that she *accidently* found herself browsing *Apartments.com* for the next hour.

***

Over the next four weeks they checked off many of the items on Nancy's list and had countless other once-in-a-lifetime experiences. The crumbled piece of paper was now creased indefinitely where they'd folded and unfolded it each time they highlighted what they'd done. Megan felt it was more personal to carry the list with them wherever they went as opposed to writing the list in her phone. The list and the small urn sat together in a black velvet pouch in Megan's rucksack.

A week in the Maldives was all the paradise Megan needed. Until they arrived Megan had always assumed the images she'd seen were photoshopped, filtered and adjusted to make them look so picturesque. There was no need. The pristine waters really were clear enough to see the nail varnish on the tips of her toes. The sands were pure and white like a dolphin's belly. The calm waters were optimal for diving, which allowed them to fulfil the diving part of the list.

The price to stay in an underwater room for the week was enough to buy a studio apartment; so that was out of the question. They opted for one night and barely slept just so they could experience it fully. The 180-degree curved acrylic dome allowed them to see out into the crystal clear water. They were within arm's reach of squirrelfish and rainbow runners—according to the brochure they were the most common fish.

Megan didn't see a shark, but she was thankful for that, because she would never be caught swimming in the water again—ever. She'd been having a reoccurring dream in the nights leading up to their stay, which was the main reason she couldn't fall asleep. In the dream, a giant great white smashed its body into the acrylic and ate them alive. This reminded her how much she hated sharks. The hotel clerk did assure them that great white sharks preferred cooler coastal waters, non-existent in the Maldives.

The next stop was a seven-hour flight to China. They spent some time in Shanghai; it was an impressive look at modern China. The skyscrapers reminded Megan of New York. Three nights was enough; the purpose of their trip was to see the ancient sights. From there they headed to Beijing. There they explored the

Forbidden City, the Temple of Heaven and the Summer Palace, before finally arriving at the Great Wall.

"I wish Gram had been a little more specific about this part. I assumed the wall was a big wall, but not thirteen thousand miles big." Megan flapped her arms, glaring at the Welcome to China sightseeing book she'd picked up at the airport. "What if she wanted to see a specific part of it?"

She zipped up the neck of her windbreaker. The changing climates were the biggest struggle on their trip. They'd gone from hot enough to burn your bare feet on the sidewalk, to cold enough to need a woolly hat. They tried to remain light on their baggage, but it was challenging choosing what to leave behind when packing.

"Thirteen thousand? Surely not?"

Megan handed Ashley the book. "It's five times the length of the United States. Clearly, I didn't listen in history."

"Wow. Well, you're not the only one. That does make sense now though," Ashley said.

"What does?"

"Well, that sign on the way in said it took two thousand years to build it. I just assumed they were slow, or it was a typo."

"I think Nancy would be disappointed in our knowledge of the seven wonders of the world," Megan joked.

"I think you're right. I don't think it matters which part we see. We're here and that's what matters." Ashley reached over and slipped her arm around Megan's waist.

They opted for the one-day guided tour in Beijing. They roamed the scenery and the mountain ridges. Step after step they climbed whilst the guide made the history around them come to life. He talked about the cost to build, the different eras it was built over and the wars that the Wall had to defend against.

As she listened intently, she imagined the type of questions Nancy would ask. Where was the first section built? Who built it? Why did they build it? Is it true people's remains are buried within the walls?

The last question was one Megan asked out of her own curiosity. She was the only person who had a question, so the guide was eager to answer.

"According to research it is calculated that over one million people died in the construction of the wall over time. Constructing the walls was hard labour. It is said that many of the bodies were buried within the walls because they lacked the manpower to dig graves for the deceased."

For the rest of the trip they looked intently at the wall for skeletal remains of any kind. It was like a historical version of I Spy.

After they'd finished exploring China, their total time spent travelling had exceeded ten weeks. The experience was one of a kind. They'd ticked off eleven of the twenty-one entries on Nancy's list. They planned to fly back to Mexico to eat at Puyol. Then they would travel from Mexico to Oregon to go truffle picking, which Megan thought was probably the most random addition to the list. However, Ashley made a good point.

"Do you not remember her famous truffle pasta? The creamy mushroom one? I can almost smell it now." Ashley sniffed the air.

"Oh God, that was the best, wasn't it? It makes sense now. Take a cooking class in Italy, learn how to make the best fettuccini and then go and pick our own truffles to make the pasta." She smiled. "Gram would've loved that."

"We will make the best truffle pasta." Ashley smiled.

Megan kissed her softly; there was no one else in the world she would rather have by her side. She didn't want their trip to end. She didn't want to return to normality. She didn't want to deal with her career complications, or worry about the little things like being late or whether the woman at the coffee shop would put too much coffee in her latte, making it impossible to drink.

The mundane things seemed so trivial now. She'd spent the last ten weeks living her life to the fullest, experiencing large parts of the world, new cultures, new surroundings and taking the time to really understand what was important.

Ashley. Family. Friends.

That was what life boiled down to: the love of a woman, the loving bond with the family you're born into and the solid foundations in which you build everlasting friendships. Those were the keys to happiness, Megan realised.

"Shall we stop off in England and see your parents before heading back?" Ashley asked.

"I would love that."

Just when Megan didn't think it was possible to be any more in love with Ashley, she would say something like that. Ashley always seemed to know what Megan needed. Her actions made Megan's heart flutter.

Megan was excited for the type of closeness that only develops over time, the type of love Christopher had felt for Nancy. He'd felt like a part of him was missing whenever Nancy wasn't there. They had been so intertwined that they almost became one person.

She watched Ashley pack her backpack in nothing but a sports bra and a tight pair of cutoff jersey shorts she'd picked up in Italy. They'd not always been cutoff. In fact, they were very much full-length until they'd arrived in India and realised it was either adapt the clothes to fit the climate or leave them behind. Ashley's hair had grown a couple of inches allowing for a messier bun. The way the odd piece fell down the back of her bare neck and landed between her toned shoulder blades was fascinating. *It's just hair*, Megan told herself. *Stop staring at her like some lovesick obsessed lunatic.*

It wasn't the first time; it wouldn't be the last.

She was lovesick.

She was obsessed.

"Come here to me, please." Megan gestured with her finger.

"Why are you looking at me like that?" Ashley laughed.

"I just really want to smell you."

"You're a lunatic." Ashley grinned. "But okay." She ran and launched herself on top of Megan. The scent of Ashley's perfume mixed with the warmth of her body and her conditioned hair was just divine.

Megan inhaled.

It seems she was a *lunatic*.

21

Ashley

They say, *when you know, you know.*

Who says that? Ashley thought. There is always a *they* involved.

That was beside the point. Ashley felt that truth; she *just knew.* It was a mixture of extremely chaotic and confusing feelings that she had absolutely no control over. At any moment of the day, she could blurt out, *I love you;* or, *I'm crazy about you;* or, *I want to suck on your earlobe until it falls off*—that one was less of an occurrence. They could be eating breakfast or washing the dishes. It didn't matter. There were times she felt like she would explode with excitement, like a volcano erupting. She couldn't control the feeling.

Ashley sat at the desk in Megan's parents' house. The same desk where she'd spent all her time writing on their first vacation to England. She had no obligation to write this time, but she wanted to. Throughout their time travelling, her journal had been firmly sandwiched in her backpack awaiting any and every moment of inspiration. It had come out often. Said inspirations, often involved love and life, and randomly one involved a crocodile and whether they had the ability to love. The way it clamped its large teeth around the unsuspecting fish, on their trip in Africa, suggested otherwise.

Ashley began contemplating what it was that made Megan so special. She felt no compulsion to hide her odd behaviours or weird tendencies around Megan—like having to stop the microwave two seconds before it finishes so it doesn't beep, or driving fast over a bridge in case it collapses. For the first time in her life, she felt like they were both equally committed to the relationship.

The idea of settling down, getting married and having kids was a future they both desperately wanted with one another. Megan fit into her life seamlessly. She knew her sister extremely well, and she got along perfectly with her best friends. The foundation had been built through years of friendship.

She made even the most boring things seem great. A walk to the local grocery store wasn't just a walk, with Megan it was a chance to laugh. Even when the wind whipped against her face, there was always a smile on it. Megan made Ashley laugh like nobody else. Emily used to be the only one who could really make her belly laugh, but Megan caused her stomach pain from the uncontrollable giggling, the terrible jokes and the hilariously accurate impressions had her in hysterics. Ashley felt completely calm and at peace in Megan's presence. For the first time she could truly say she was genuinely happy.

All of the above led her to one decision that was more exciting than it was scary.

The proposal.

Was it too soon? She'd asked Emily the day before. Her response had been typical, "Put a ring on the girl's finger before she leaves you. She's a ten and you're a nine and a half. " There was no arguing with that. Megan was a ten. If anything, Ashley was quite flattered by Emily's nine and a half. Jason had agreed. According to him, no time was too soon. He also had a hidden agenda. She was very much aware he wanted her bedroom; so there was that.

Ashley was afraid of being seen as the girl who proposed to everyone she fell in love with and got left at the altar. She supposed it was better than getting divorced, but it was not ideal. The anxiety crept in whenever she thought about the sheer amount of money that had been wasted on her almost wedding to Madison. She was positive that Julie would require some sort of money-back guarantee on the catering at the next one, assuming she'd contribute at all. Maybe she had a one-wedding policy.

When Ashley spotted Michael coming in from his morning run, she saw her opportunity. Ashley slipped her hand into the pocket of her sweatpants; there she felt the little square box that she'd been hiding since India. The box provided by the jewellers was too big, so she'd sourced a small black circular box from a different jeweller. That allowed her to hide it perfectly in her luggage.

It was a risk to go through customs with a piece of jewellery worth more than $2,000. The fear of being stopped and searched and her whole plan being ruined caused her to sweat. She worried that it made her look guilty. It could raise suspicion that she was some sort of drug mule carrying bags of cocaine in the lining of her backpack. Luckily, the guy at the airport seemed way more interested in chatting up his fellow colleague than paying attention to what was in her bag. At the time that didn't fill her with confidence for their trip.

She reached the bottom of the stairs and composed herself, one deep breath, then another, before sharply rounding the corner into the kitchen.

Michael instantly jumped backwards into a Karate Kid type stance. Ashley held her hands up, as if she was being held at gunpoint. "I come in peace." She grinned.

"Jesus, Ashley. You nearly gave me a heart attack." He removed his headphones; the noise cancellation meant that his verbal response was loud enough to wake up the entire house.

"Sssshhh." Ashley touched her finger to her lips and listened for any movement upstairs.

"Are you telling me to shush in my own home?" Michael raised his eyebrow.

"No . . . technically yes . . . but for good reason." She gestured towards the kitchen. This wasn't the way she'd planned it.

"You want me to go in the kitchen?"

"Yes please," she pleaded. It was now or never.

"Can I at least get my protein shake?" Michael asked.

Ashley nodded. She sat on the chair at one side of the island waiting patiently.

Tap, tap, tap, her fingers drummed on the marble work surface. The window of opportunity was getting smaller, and Michael was interested in adding exactly fifty grams of chocolate protein powder to his milk. When he started to distribute his numerous bottles of vitamin tablets into sections like some pharmacist, she had to hurry him along.

"Michael . . ."

He turned towards her. "Why do you look so nervous, Ashley?"

Because you're making me nervous, she thought. If only he would sit down and listen to her, she could stop sweating like a Christmas turkey.

"I need to speak with you before Megan wakes up."

"Do you owe someone money?" He raised his eyebrow. "Please don't tell me someone got you to smuggle something whilst you were travelling?" He jested.

She rolled her eyes. Clearly, she did look like the smuggling type.

"No, of course not."

"Oh good." Michael breathed a sigh of relief. "Sorry, go ahead. I'm all ears."

Finally, she thought. She glanced around the room, intentionally avoiding eye contact. Her posture screamed uncomfortable, and the more she thought about how nervous she was the worse the feeling became.

Ashley coughed and cleared her throat. "You know I love your daughter."

Michael nodded.

"Well, I have been thinking for a while now about our future. Megan means the world to me, and I hope to spend the rest of my life proving that to her." Ashley reached into her pocket and pulled out the black box.

"I would like to ask your daughter to marry me. I was hoping that you would give me your blessing."

The word *blessing* came out as a whisper. She looked down at her hands, nervously fidgeting with the box. She hoped Michael would break the silence between them. When she saw his silhouette stand, she feared the worst. It wasn't until he rounded the side of the island and reached out to hug her that she realised he wasn't about to say *no*.

"You can 1000% have my blessing, Ashley." He smiled and pointed towards the box. "Is this the ring?" Ashley nodded. "May I see it?"

She opened the box. Inside was the most perfect oval cut diamond ring. One gleaming diamond solitaire sat elegantly on a white gold band. The simplicity of the classic solitaire ring made it even more beautiful.

"That's beautiful," Michael said. "Where did you get it?"

"In India. We passed a jeweller in New Delhi. It was lit up in the window, sparkling on this circular blue stand. It looked incredible. Megan hinted that one day if she ever got married, she would love a ring like that. I went back and bought it the next morning."

There was a bang upstairs. Ashley instinctively snapped the box shut and shoved it in her pocket.

"When are you going to ask her?" Michael asked.

"I don't know yet. I think I will know when the time is right." She smiled.

"I'm sure you will. I won't tell Amanda because she cannot keep a secret, and she'll act all weird around Meg. Believe me when I say, you have both of our blessings." Amanda was known to spill the beans on almost all occasions; so that was the safer option.

"That means so much, thank you."

"I have never seen my daughter so happy. During the hardest time of her life, you made her happy. She wouldn't have survived those months after her accident without you, Ashley. I don't know if I have ever thanked you for that." Michael squeezed her shoulder. Then he made his way back to the opposite side of the kitchen to his vitamins. They pretended the conversation had never happened, as Megan walked through the doorway.

Now, Ashley needed to find the time to plan her proposal. Sending Megan to a basketball game with Michael might give her some time, the cogs began turning.

***

The proposal.

It was never easy to summon the courage to ask for someone's hand in marriage. Yes, Ashley had done it once before, but that made her no more experienced than the next person. This proposal was different. Ashley had no doubts. Megan was the one.

The fear came from knowing wholeheartedly that Megan was her endgame. She was the final touchdown in the Superbowl and the buzzer-beater at the end of the fourth quarter in the WNBA finals. Ashley couldn't imagine a life *after* Megan.

When she considered how she would propose, the idea of writing little love notes made the most sense to her. She was a writer. It should come naturally; that had been her initial thought. The mess of scribbles, crossed out words, sentences and paragraph after paragraph of crumpled drafts contradicted the simplicity of her plan. The words eventually made their way from pen to paper, but nothing seemed to capture the depth of love she felt for Megan.

The plan was to do it privately. They'd spoken about grand gestures; they weren't Megan's preferred style. She would say no if proposed to in a basketball stadium filled with seventy thousand fans, for example. That had been duly noted. They'd travelled to so many amazing places in the past three months, any one of them could have been a perfect setting, but Ashley had wanted to be traditional in a sense. She wanted to see Michael face to face and ask him for his daughter's hand. She figured it was also harder to say no to someone sat in front of you crying like a nervous wreck.

Michael would take his daughter to the local basketball game on Friday night, giving Ashley at least three hours to set the scene.

When they arrived home a series of clues and riddles would take her to the barn where Ashley would be waiting.

The last remaining thing that she couldn't plan or foresee was her answer.

Yes? No?

22

Megan

The nostalgia that came when watching basketball with her father was overwhelming for Megan. For so many years they'd gone to games, the level didn't matter. They adored the sport. It was in their DNA. It haunted her that she might never play again. She'd had enough distractions in recent months to put her worries to the back of her mind, but when the world fell silent, usually at night, she still thought about her lost hopes and dreams. She wondered if it would ever get easier. Then she thought about what could have been: the chance of death, her grandmother. That's when she told herself there was more to life than basketball. Even if it didn't feel that way.

The Newcastle Eagles were playing the Cheshire Phoenix. It was a highly anticipated BBL trophy quarter-final game. The game was exhilarating from start to finish. With every crashing rebound, Megan jumped forwards. Her eyes zoned in on the shooters arms each time they went up for a three. She knew instantly if it was going to drop. If it didn't, she was already looking for the defender.

Who was getting the rebound?

Who was boxing out?

Who was the outlet?

Her mind was on to the next play. Like a video game, she was desperately willing the players to stand in the positions she wanted them in, to drive when there was an opening, to step back and to shoot when the defender was shorter or a second too late to the mark.

When the power forward for the Cheshire Phoenix backed the defender into the paint then dropped his shoulder to get to the rim, it was a thing of beauty—the reverse layup for a big man was pretty.

"Switch to zone. Switch to zone," Megan yelled. "He always goes right . . . watch your weak side, number eight."

She threw her arms out towards the opposing team's centre. "What are you guarding him for? He can barely shoot . . . watch out for the cut!"

Megan flung her left arm out getting her dad's attention by hitting him in the chest. "Have you noticed they only send number three in for the offensive boards?"

"Yep, bad move."

Megan noticed the family in front of them turning every time she screamed orders. She'd become that person, the one in the crowd at a sporting event that doesn't shut up, but she knew what she was talking about. The young boy was finding it amusing.

"Box him out!" She jumped up again.

"Take that charge number ten! Yes!"

Michael smirked.

"What?" Megan said.

"Nothing. I just think you'd make a good coach, for what it's worth."

Her basketball IQ was higher than most; she'd been told that all through college basketball and into her professional years. The coaches often praised her on her in-game decision making, her ability to lead and her "scary-ass yelling" when the team needed it most.

Maybe she would make a good coach, she thought. The idea became more appealing the more she came to terms with her future in basketball.

"Maybe," she replied.

"Oh, come on. Even I don't notice some of the things you see, and I have been a fan of this game a hell of a lot longer. You were an incredibly talented player. You could be an incredibly talented coach if it's what you want to do. I know you can."

"Thanks dad."

Her attention turned immediately back to the game. "Come on ref, you're killing me!"

The woman in front of them almost dropped her hot dog. Megan's dad burst out laughing.

***

They returned home two hours later. It was almost 7:00 p.m. The night sky had turned black. The stars were visible, as her dad had pointed out on numerous occasions. He'd even offered to pull over so she could look at them—that was the weird part. She noticed his phone light up once or twice, and he was quick to dismiss the messages.

What was he up to? Megan thought.

When they walked through the front door, there was a large bouquet of red roses on the console table. They hadn't been there when she'd left.

"Treating mom again?" She turned towards her dad.

"They're not from me."

"Oh." Megan was confused now. As she got closer and examined the card, it read.

Roses are red . . . joking.

You told me once your dream bouquet was fifty red roses. So, I got you fifty-one because I promise to always exceed your expectations.

Go to the kitchen.

The flowers were a perfect deep shade of red, and they sat tightly in a circular black box.

"They're pretty." Michael smirked and made his way upstairs.

On the kitchen counter she spied a mojito, to the right of it another note. There was no sign of Ashley.

The note read.

Meeting you for the first time was electrifying. I instantly knew you were special, but it wasn't until our first date when I watched you sip your Mojito and glare intently at me that I knew I would never be able to forget those eyes. You saw straight into my soul, and I didn't realise at the time just how rare that was.

Head to the basketball court outside.

Megan carried her drink with her; the Mojito had been made to perfection with a skilful blend of mint and sugar. The lights above the basketball court were already on.

"Ash?"

No response.

In the centre of the court lay a basketball. There was no note this time. Instead, the note had been written in black marker on the ball. She placed her drink on the ground and began rotating the ball to find the beginning.

It's no secret that basketball was your life. Just like the bounce of this ball was your favourite sound, your laugh is mine. Just like you couldn't imagine your life without basketball, I can't imagine mine without you. I hope with time I can be your basketball the way that you are mine.

Join me in the stable. Fred has something to say.

Megan's eyes filled as she approached the stable; the lights were on inside. She saw her beautiful shire horse Fred.

"Hey big fella, how are you?"

She kissed the smooth part of his face between his nostrils and his mouth. She gently stroked his mane. He had his coat on, attached to the coat was another note.

We haven't had the easiest journey, or the most traditional. One or two obstacles caused us to veer off course, but despite the odds being stacked against us at times, we found our way back to each other. There hasn't been a day gone by since I met you that I haven't thought about you.

I never want to stop stupidly smiling at my phone whenever you text. I never want to wake up without you by my side. I want your voice to be the only one I hear every morning and every night. I never believed in soulmates before you, but I am here now with you because you made me believe. Every choice I have made in my life has led me here, to you.

There is no one else in this world I want to do life with. The good, the bad, the ugly. I want it all with you. That leads me to the final part, a question . . .

Megan heard the barn door close behind her. She turned to find Ashley on one knee.

"No . . ." Megan inhaled.

"You're saying no?" Ashley's eyes widened.

"God no . . ."

"God, no?" Ashley's brow furrowed.

"Shit . . . I mean *God no* to me saying no. I'm sorry."

Ashley remained on one knee, yet to reveal the ring.

"This is not the response I was hoping for," Ashley said.

"I wanted to propose to you! I was planning on proposing to you," Megan covered her face with her hands.

"You were?"

"Yes! I have the ring in the house." Megan stepped towards her, she too knelt on one knee. "You beat me to it," she whispered.

"Can I ask the question now?" Ashley grinned.

"Wait . . . can I get the ring for you?"

Megan set off lightly jogging towards the main house before Ashley had chance to respond. Just before she reached the door, her father appeared at the window. He dropped the box containing the ring down from the second floor.

"How did you? Never mind."

Within seconds Megan was back in front of Ashley, who hadn't changed her position.

"This isn't quite how I planned this proposal," Ashley joked.

"Me either."

"On three?" Ashley held the box outstretched, and Megan did the same. She couldn't contain the grin on her face; it felt like a dream. The woman she wanted to marry wanted to marry her too.

"Will you marry me?" they said in unison, both rings were revealed to the other at the same time. Megan noticed the diamond instantly. "Is that?"

"The one in India? Yes."

Megan cried happy tears.

"Is that a, yes?" Ashley asked.

"Yes, yes, yes." She held out her left hand as Ashley slid on the diamond ring; it was the perfect fit. She'd forgotten one all important thing, "You haven't said yes to me." Megan sniffled, she was ugly crying now, which was embarrassing, but she didn't care.

"As if you need to ask. Yes, 1000% I will marry you." Ashley beamed.

Megan removed the ring from the box, it was also a solitaire diamond ring, the cut was square as opposed to oval like the one she now possessed.

Ashley had never hinted at what style of ring she would like, so when Megan went to choose one with her dad a few days earlier she expected the trip to be a long one. Until she saw the emerald cut ring shining in the window display. It was all-encompassing. It lit up the display, and no other ring in its vicinity compared— it reminded her of Ashley.

"It's beautiful," Ashley said.

"Yeah? I wasn't sure if you'd like it. I hoped you would." Megan lowered her gaze.

"It's perfect, Meg." Ashley reached out and pulled Megan to her feet. Fred gave a celebratory neigh which made them both laugh.

"Well, at least we have Fred's approval." Megan chuckled.

They sealed the proposal with a kiss. It was passionate, and it satisfied Megan to the core.

"I could live off that," Megan whispered.

The excitement had distracted her so much she didn't even notice the table set up in the corner, a romantic candlelit dinner for two.

"Your mom helped me prepare dinner. She'll bring it out when we're ready."

"You told my mom?" Megan looked surprised.

"Oh no, not until two hours ago when I knew she couldn't ruin the surprise." Ashley pointed out.

"Poor mom." Megan laughed. "But definitely the right choice."

In that moment she understood the meaning of—*diamonds are a girl's best friend*—she watched her ring sparkle as she got used to the feeling on her finger.

This is it, Megan thought.

The feeling of knowing you've found your person. She'd always known it, deep down, but now, somehow, as materialistic as it seemed, the ring proved the knowing. It signified the bond between them and their desire to build a life together. It clarified what she'd known in her heart all along.

"When did you know?" Megan asked.

"That I wanted to marry you?"

"Yes."

"I have known since the moment I met you," Ashley revealed. "I just lost my way a little."

"I love you." Megan's lips edged closer to Ashley's face once again.

"I love you too, Megan Davis."

She pulled Ashley's hand towards her lips, brushing a light kiss against her finger, then she kissed her cheek, her eyes, her nose, until finally their lips locked once again and all that was left to do was savour the moment.

23

Ashley
One Month Later

"Jason, I know you're desperate for me to move out, but I didn't think you'd literally be accompanying us house-hunting."

They entered the first apartment, one of five they'd planned to view that morning.

"Honey, yes, I want your apartment; yes, I have an ulterior motive being here today, but regardless, I am the one with the most interior design experience in this group. I also plan to spend a lot of my time in whatever apartment you choose. My being here is as beneficial to me as it is to you."

"Noted." Ashley laughed. Jason had previously worked for a house staging company in his early twenties. He'd lasted six months.

"Like what is this place? Why is it so dull? And the artwork . . . ugh . . . it's making me nauseous."

The realtor was instantly offended. Ashley could tell by the realtors expressions that the last thing he wanted when he'd opted to show two lesbians a bunch of apartments, was their two gay best friends to tag along. One was obscenely opinionated on the décor. The other did all of the annoying parental things, like checking the taps, making sure the toilets flushed and asking questions like, "Where does the garbage go?" Or, "When does the routine maintenance take place?"

If it had walls, floors, windows and didn't smell like rotting corpses or sewage, Ashley was happy to consider it.

Emily strolled in, she'd been lingering outside, probably checking the stairwell for infestation, Ashley thought.

"I asked the neighbour what it was like around here at night. She said it's quiet. So, that's good. She also suggested a new bar on the corner of 56th—great for cocktails, apparently, and it's just down the road which makes for an easy drunken stroll home." Emily appeared happy with herself.

"Shall we just leave?" Megan joked.

"I don't think we're needed here," Ashley whispered as Emily began dramatically tapping at the walls.

"What about bed bugs?" Jason quizzed the young, suited realtor.

"Already checked!" Emily yelled before he had the chance to respond. "I put it in on the Bedbug Registry, we're all clear."

Ashley covered her mouth to hide her amusement. "Do they think this is some dive? It's a nice apartment on 57th and 5th!"

Megan intertwined their fingers and squeezed reassuringly. "Who cares. Let them ask all the boring questions. You know what I want to see?" She raised her eyebrows suggestively.

"What?"

"The bedroom." Megan pulled her towards the other end of the apartment.

"The cell phone reception is good too, Ash," Emily said.

"Good to know," Ashley's voice trailed off. She mouthed silently at the realtor, "I'm sorry."

The bedroom had four white walls with floor to ceiling windows on one wall. A large wooden bed was backed against the largest wall. A huge black and white abstract painting, that Ashley immediately loved, hung over the headboard. The main bedroom had an en-suite and two sets of double wardrobes.

"I love it," Ashley said. "I know it's on the higher end of our budget, but it's so nice."

"I agree. I could see us in here." She closed the door softly behind her. "Walking from the en-suite to the bed, completely naked. Maybe I'll be looking for my underwear in these drawers here." She bent over, although she was playing around, Ashley couldn't take her eyes off her; she was sexy and seductive even when she was joking.

"I like the sound of that. Anything else you might want to do in this room?" Ashley grinned, sitting back on the edge of the bed.

"I can think of a thing or two." Megan winked. She walked over and stood in between her legs. There was an intentional placement of her thigh which excited Ashley. Megan towered over her, slowly pushing her body back onto the bed. Ashley let her neck roll backwards as Megan showered it with kisses.

Next, they heard Emily bellow from the corridor and jumped to their feet.

"To be continued?" Megan smirked.

"You bet." Ashley gestured towards the blinds as Jason and Emily entered the room followed swiftly by the realtor.

"These are great . . . and the bed looks super comfortable as well. I assume the furniture in here comes with the apartment?" Ashley knew the answer but was trying desperately to pretend they hadn't almost been caught making out.

"Yes, as I said to your friends here. Everything in the house is included, that's why it's listed as fully furnished." He turned on his heel and wandered across the hall to the second bedroom.

"Ewwww," Jason mocked, before jogging behind him pretending to grab his butt. The handsome realtor was completely oblivious to Jason's derogatory advances.

Emily wandered past Ashley and pointed towards the bed. "Looks a little crinkled; testing it out, were we?"

Ashley blushed. Emily should've been a detective.

***

Apartment hunting had taken its toll on them. They'd hit five apartments in three hours. Their second pit stop of the day was for a coffee to refuel before they tackled the rest of Saturday afternoon. Ashley's plan was for herself and Megan to go out and celebrate Megan's new job, but it turned into the four of them before Sofia invited herself, making it five. She was almost certain the number would grow by the time evening came around.

"So, apartment one or three? That's the question." Jason dropped into the booth beside Emily, signalling for the waitress to come and take their order.

"Jason, you can't call someone over like that, it's rude," Ashley pointed out.

"Honey, she works for me at the bar every Saturday night. I know her, it's cool. Chill." He said whilst glaring over the top of his sunglasses.

Thank God, Ashley thought. The girl was now less likely to spit in their coffee.

"I think apartment one." She turned towards Megan gripping her thigh beneath the table. "What about you, babe?"

"I think the first one as well. It fits the budget, it's quiet and the amenities are good. The neighbours seem nice, and the decor was so nice. It being fully furnished is ideal as well. It saves us buying everything. We might as well save all that for when we buy our own place in the future."

"Agreed," Ashley said.

Jason sat forwards with his head in his hands, the picture of a man about to lovingly roast his friends. "You two . . . I just can't."

"What?" Megan laughed.

"You're just really fucking cute. I thought Ashley and Madison were cute, but this." He waved back and forth between them. "This is something else."

The booth fell silent. Ashley glanced awkwardly between Megan and Emily, who now sat gawking at Jason.

"You're an idiot." Emily whacked him in the arm.

"What did I say?"

The Madison subject was a tricky one. There was no denying that Ashley hoped to one day be friends with her again. The bond they had spanned decades. There were things she'd experienced with Madison that she would never forget, memorable times that she would one day tell her children about.

The question Ashley asked herself was, would her children know her as *Auntie Maddie*? They'd once had dreams of growing up, marrying the loves of their lives, living on the same street and going on vacations with their families together as one. They dreamt as children that they would always be the best of friends, even re-enacting a platonic version of wedding vows. Until death do us part, they'd said. Maybe this was just an example of for better or worse. Maybe they could work out how to be in each other's lives again.

"Is this about Madison? Oh, come on, haven't you two kissed and made up yet?" Jason really wasn't making things any better.

"There will be no kissing," Megan clarified. "But . . ." Everyone paused, waiting in suspense. "I'm not opposed to you trying to rebuild your friendship."

"Really?" Ashley raised her eyebrow, suspicious.

"Yes. I know how important she is to you."

"How did you end up with this one? She's literally a saint," Jason said.

"Oh, I don't know about that." Megan looked intently at the pattern on the surface of her coffee.

"Oh yeah? What naughty sins have you committed then?" Jason winked.

"Wouldn't you like to know."

Ashley placed her arm around Megan's shoulder. She leaned in.

Find someone who trusts you wholeheartedly and only wants the very best for you. Find someone who compliments your aura, someone who brings positivity and light into your life, someone who above all else makes you want to be a better person.

Ashley had finally found her.

24

Megan
Two Months Later

It was the middle of summer. June had seen temperatures plateau at eighty-five degrees Fahrenheit, but July had reared its ugly head; temperatures in excess of ninety degrees Fahrenheit seemed to be a daily occurrence. Luckily, they'd opted for the apartment with a good air-conditioning unit—Emily had made sure of that.

There were places to hide in New York where the sun wouldn't bear down on you. That was a benefit of being surrounded by skyscrapers. The downside was the humidity. The weather woman made it clear every morning just how much worse it was getting. Megan felt bad for not having the same enthusiasm towards preventing climate change that Greta Thunberg had. Instead, she wore less, and paid more in utility bills throughout the summer months. She left the climate maintenance to others.

The minute she left the apartment, she removed her tracksuit jacket. She wore a training t-shirt. It had a thinner back-panel that allowed the air to circulate, so she didn't end up looking like a sweaty mess before she even entered the gym. The walk to her new place of work in Upper Manhattan was only fifteen minutes. She could call that her way of helping the planet.

The need to take public transport had diminished, thankfully. The only place hotter than the streets of New York in the summer was the New York underground.

The blue lion on her tracksuit jacket indicated the Columbia Lions. The Ivy League school, founded in 1754, was her first appointment as head coach. The previous coach had taken an offer to work overseas. The NCAA team had endured a series of unsuccessful seasons spanning a decade, four different coaches and numerous talented athletes leaving for bigger programmes which left them in a position to rebuild. When Cheryl called with options, Megan hadn't expected to receive offers for anything other than assistant head coach for her first appointment. Naturally, her nerves skyrocketed the moment she accepted.

There were no number of coaching manifestos and self-help books that would prepare her for the role. Before she walked through the door on her first day, she'd spent weeks upon weeks observing film.

Her aim was to build a championship programme. She gave a speech on the first day about the credentials needed to be a Columbia Lions player. She wanted players with grit, determination, toughness and versatility; players that played with fierce competitiveness. She wanted to see 110% effort day in and day out. *Work hard, play hard,* was the motto already etched on the wall in her new office.

They were three months away from the start of the 2021 season. It was summer break for most college students, but being a D1 athlete was different. For them, there was no summer around the pool, eating mom's homemade pastries and soaking up the sun. Many of the athletes lived in New York. They helped on campus with training camps. They were provided with strict summer workout schedules, along with a workout partner to communicate with throughout the summer months.

Megan used the summer to scout incoming talent, to observe the training camps and most importantly, to see who had the determination she was looking for. She noted who would turn up to practice three times a week, in sweltering heat when they had every right to be at the beach. She wanted to be impressed, and it seemed they wanted to impress her too; for the third week in a row much of the team had turned up for a no-obligation practice.

"Why are you here?" Megan yelled at the group.

"To train, coach," the tall centre forward known as *Landy* responded.

"Really?"

"Yes, coach," another player yelled.

Megan looked them all in the eyes individually. "You could have fooled me."

She placed her hands forwards awaiting the ball toss from the team's point guard. "Let me be clear. I will push you harder than anyone's ever pushed you because I believe in this team. I believe in your ability, and I know you can succeed."

They stood with their heads bowed. "When I first stepped foot in this gym, what was my vow to you?"

The team stood in silence.

"Did I not tell you that we would make this team the best it has ever been?"

"Yes, coach," they roared.

"I need each one of you to be locked in to achieve that. You must have the same mindset as me."

She bounced the ball once.

"Every practice is a chance to get better."

Twice.

"Preparation is what wins games."

Three times.

"I don't want to see another half-assed attempt at going up for a board. If you can't get the offensive rebound, then we lose the second chance points."

Another bounce.

"Grab the damn ball . . . I don't care if this is pre-season. We treat every practice like it's a championship game. Do you hear me?"

"Yes, coach!"

"I need your effort. I need your blood, sweat and tears. When your legs feel like they're going to buckle, I need you to find the strength to power through. When you complain that your arms are hurting because you've practiced shooting for two hours straight, you continue for another hour." Megan shot the ball from her standing position. The three-point shot fell smoothly. She was extremely grateful. A miss would've been embarrassing and contradicted the speech she was giving. "Pass me another."

The point guard retrieved another ball and launched it towards Megan. One quick catch and shoot, another swish. It was effortless.

"I'm not warmed up. I'm not in the flow of a game. Hell, I haven't played competitively for over a year. So, how do I hit that shot so easily?"

They looked towards each other. The answer seemed simple enough, but the uncertainty was obvious. "You're just really good," Landy said.

"Wrong."

"Luck," the team's three-point specialist jested. The shooting guard was good, but she was cocky. Megan had learned that if you're cocky, your work ethic must match that confidence.

She smirked. "Hit me again." The third shot fell just as easily as the first two. No hesitation.

"I can go all day. It isn't because I have a god given talent. It isn't luck. The reason I can hit that shot in my sleep is because of my muscle memory. When you train more than you sleep, you'll understand. It pays to play through the pain. It pays to shoot shots whilst the world is still asleep. It pays to practice hard because every single day is a chance to be better. I'm assuming you want to get better?"

"Yes, coach."

"I'm assuming you want to have the chance to be champions? To maybe play in the WNBA one day?"

"Yes, coach," the combined response grew louder, more aggressive.

"Good. Are you ready to become the best versions of yourselves?"

"Yes, coach," the team yelled.

Megan raised her hand. The team followed suit. "On three."

"One . . . two . . . three . . ." Megan chanted.

"LIONS."

Megan knew what it took to be the best. The work ethic, the consistency and the self-discipline. She'd lived that life. The early mornings, the late nights, the missed social events, replacing a pizza with a nutritional smoothie and being the first to enter the gym and the last to leave. That had been her life for so many years; it was still her life to a degree. She struggled to sleep in and often stayed after practice to use the empty gym to get her shots up. With each one that fell her heart argued with her head.

Could she have made it back?

Maybe, in another lifetime, she thought.

The benefit of not having basketball consume her entire being was that it allowed more quality time with Ashley. She was her saving grace.

25

Ashley
One year later

A summer wedding, blue skies and an outdoor setting that would soon highlight the sunset. The venue was intended to be intimate, close friends and family only. Four rows of seating positioned at either side of a white flower covered aisle were just enough to accommodate their limited guest list.

A large oak tree towered over the grassy area. There were lanterns hanging from the branches. Each held a scented candle. The guests were treated to a signature sangria station on arrival. Complimentary fans with the date and their names engraved on the handles lay in a wicker basket by the aisle. The planning had involved a discussion on how to help their guests battle the heat that was inevitable with a New York summer, whilst quenching their thirst. Ashley felt pleased with the outcome as she watched their nearest and dearest compliment the arrangements.

The surroundings were perfectly green with the right amount of white to compliment the aesthetic. The only colour came from the pink hanging blooms; they were subtle, but enough to catch guests' attention. They'd opted against using Victoria; she was good, but Ashley figured using the same planner as her first almost wedding had to be bad luck.

Ashley wandered around the venue. In fewer than twenty minutes she would marry the woman of her dreams. She took the time to take it all in. The alfresco dining arrangements looked unbelievably beautiful. The Italian garden party look had been achieved perfectly by the planners. The main building's outside wall was almost reminiscent of the Italian stone they'd seen on the farmhouses in Tuscany. That had been the ultimate selling point of this location for both of them. Paired with the low-cut shrubs, the overhead wooden lanterns and the delicate twinkle lights, that she'd been informed would transform the evening, everything came together to create a picturesque event.

It was everything they'd hoped for and more. Neither of them wanted extravagant. They opted for minimalistic. It was a personal feel that gave them the confidence that the people present wanted nothing but the very best for them. Their close-knit group of guests were there to witness a celebration of love.

Over the past year Ashley and Madison had managed to mend their friendship. It wasn't easy at first, but eventually, they fell back into their familiar ways. The ease in which Megan, Emily and Jason accepted the renewed friendship allowed things to flow naturally. Madison sat beside Emily at Ashley and Megan's wedding. She smiled so genuinely that Ashley knew in that moment that there was no longer a shred of animosity, only a joint love and respect for one another's happiness.

Today was about Ashley and Megan; it was about their future, their shared commitment to one another, and it was a celebration of love. Ashley would forever call that love her greatest gift in life.

The Vows.

In remembrance of Nancy, Megan used the vows Nancy had written in her final letter. Each word of the vows she'd said to Christopher all those years ago, rang true. Ashley glanced at Christopher and watched him dab the handkerchief to his face remembering the love he had for his late wife. It was a touching tribute that brought the guests to tears.

There was just one small part that Megan added on at the end.

"Ash, I love you. I have always loved you. Even when we were worlds apart. I always carried you with me. Ever since the day I met you, my heart has only known one thing, and that's you. The odds felt stacked against us at times, but I never lost faith in my feelings for you. I asked the universe to make me believe in fate, and it delivered. You are my destiny, today, tomorrow and forever."

Ashley's eyes glazed over. She smiled softly and whispered, "I love you," in return.

She reached for the folded piece of paper that had been neatly tucked away in her pocket since she purchased the suit. Finding the words to express her love and gratitude towards Megan didn't come easily. Every sentence had at first felt like an injustice to their love story, and she was conscious of undermining the significance of the connection they shared. Eventually she allowed her heart to lead the way, and the words merged together to create something special.

"The first moment I laid eyes on you, I felt this surge of electricity through my whole body. It sounds cliché, but it's true. Your smile kick-started my heart. Your presence made me feel alive for the first time. Before you I was just existing; I didn't realise what it felt like to really live. You consumed my every thought after that day. I dreamt of the moment I would see you again, night after night, and each morning as I woke, I wondered if you would return to me. Eventually you did, and the world made sense again. A love like ours makes you vulnerable. It makes you do crazy things, but when trusted it will always prevail. I promise from here on out to always put you first. I promise to make you laugh every single day. I promise to never leave your side, and to always remember that the love we share is extraordinary and incomparable. You consume me. You matchlessly amaze me, and if there is one thing in life I am certain of, it is that I will love you forever."

Megan dabbed at her eyes with the tissue provided by the minister; she was prepared. Megan reached for the silver band and placed it upon Ashley's finger at the request of the Minister.

"Do you, Ashley Stewart, take Megan Davis to be your lawfully wedded wife?"

"I do," Ashley said, without hesitation. In response, Ashley held Megan's ring in place, hovering over the tip of Megan's perfectly manicured fingernails.

"And do you Meg . . ."

"I do," Megan interrupted. The guest's laughter echoed through the air.

"I think you're supposed to wait until she finishes the sentence," Ashley whispered.

"Sorry . . ." The minister was a family friend, so she wasn't about to banish her to an eternity of misery in hell. "I have waited long enough for you. I don't want to wait any longer."

Ashley squeezed her hand tighter. They were surrounded by friends and family, with eyes watching their every move, but to Ashley it felt as though they were alone. Together, hand in hand, their eyes fixated on only each other; the world around them fell away.

Ashley had been told to cherish every moment of her wedding day. Her mother, on reflection of her own wedding day, had informed Ashley just how quickly it came and went. She'd advised them to focus on each other in the moment and on the reason they were there. It was surprisingly the first nice thing her mother had said in reference to a wedding since the split from her father. She half expected a protest to take place—her mom chained to the large oak tree unwilling to let her daughter make the same mistakes she had—thankfully her mother sat in the front row, beaming and seemingly unphased by Benjamin's presence.

"Shall I continue?" Minister Sally smirked.

"Yes please," Megan said, but her eyes never left Ashley's.

"By the power vested in me, I now pronounce you wife and wife. You may now kiss your bride."

"Finally." Megan breathed a sigh of relief.

Suddenly, the nerves faded. Ashley welcomed Megan's lips upon hers; they were the most soft perfectly fitting lips that she vowed to kiss for the rest of her life.

The guests applauded as the pianist smoothly ran his fingers along the piano keys; the opening line of "Turning Page" by Sleeping at Last, started their walk back down the aisle. The videographer manoeuvred around them with skill, capturing the falling confetti, the sun setting in the background and the smiles of their guests. Ashley observed her bride, the way the strands of hair fell onto her face. Her smile was large and genuine, capturing the essence of the day. The dress draped from Megan's body like it was an extension of her; they moved in unison without obstruction.

Ashley knew that Megan would look spectacular, but she had never had anyone physically take her breath away.

The money shot at the end of the aisle saw them stop and kiss once more, hand in hand, with smiles so wide Ashley started to lose sensation in her cheeks; it was a feeling she hoped she'd never stop feeling.

***

"The euphoria of falling in love eclipsed all my expectations. Marrying the woman of my dreams was exhilarating, but I know now that falling in love isn't the only key to happiness.

"It is the start of a long journey, one of self-realisation, of endurance, but most importantly of sacrifice and commitment. The feeling of being in love consumes us; it hijacks all rational thought and reason.

"It's simply thrilling.

"When falling in love fades you realise that staying in love is the most important thing. That is when you look beyond the passionate highs of a newly budding relationship, and you focus on long-term stability, the consistent affection, the understanding and trust.

"I don't just love my wife, I like her too. She is my best friend, and I am hers. I once heard that love deeply rooted in friendship creates true happiness.

"She brings out the best in me; she brings me great joy, constant laughter and comfort in her company.

"We will spend our lives sharing in mutual joy and being apprehensive together in our mutual fear, because life is far from perfect.

"Laid before us are numerous decades of life together and I am confident in the knowledge that our love and friendship can conquer all."

Ashley finished reading the final paragraph of her latest article.

"You wrote that for me?" Megan said. She stood from her seated position on the bed and wandered to the desk in the corner where Ashley often typed away. She wrapped her arms around her shoulders. "It's beautiful."

"Just like you." Ashley leant back and placed a kiss on her lips.

"What now?" Megan nodded towards the article.

"What do you mean?"

"What's next?"

"With us?" Ashley questioned.

Megan nodded. "Friendship, love, a home, marriage . . ." She pointed out. "There's only one thing left."

Ashley jumped to the obvious conclusion. "You're ready for that?" She raised her eyebrows.

Megan caressed Ashley's stomach.

"I'm ready for everything with you."

Thank you for reading *If We Meet Again—The Choice.* I hope you enjoyed it.

Want to stay updated with news about my books?

Follow me on Instagram: **@nss_writings**

Follow me on Twitter: **@NicoleSkillen**

Like me on Facebook: **NicoleSpencerSkillen**

And if you have a moment, please take the time to review *If We Meet Again—The Choice.* I would be eternally grateful.

Thank you once more for your support, and I hope we meet again between the pages of another book.

ABOUT THE AUTHOR

Nicole Spencer-Skillen is a best-selling author of Sapphic Romance novels and a die-hard LA Lakers fan. She is incredibly passionate about writing novels with relatable, funny and emotionally compelling LGBT+ characters.

Born and raised in Lancashire, England, she has aspirations of surfing rooftop bars and ice-skating in Central Park, whilst living out her dream career in New York City.

Printed in Great Britain
by Amazon

20047779R00150